SIX KIPPERS

An Orcadian Adventure.

by

Anthony Bryant

Contents

PREFACE

THIS STORY IS FICTION! So all the people are fictional, including those with Orkney names, (and one Shetland one), I hope no one is offended.

Treasures of Scotland is my invention, and just because I have drawn on my experience with the National Trust for Scotland and have some knowledge of Historic Scotland, do not assume that I am reflecting them, anyone in them or the way they work.

The places and monuments in Orkney mentioned do of course exist (all but one) and are as described, and their importance is recognised by World Heritage status. They are wonderful; a visit is highly recommended. Historic Scotland looks after most of the larger ones in 'real life' except for St Magnus Cathedral, which belongs to the people of Orkney, even though used by the Church of Scotland. A number of smaller sites are owned and looked after by the owners of the farms where they stand. One of the benefits of this is that visitors can see them just as they are. An example is the Tomb of the Eagles; you see it as it is; and go in pulling yourself on a trolley. No one tells you what to do, or forbids you on health and safety grounds.

New finds come to light all the time. The excavation of the Ness of Brodgar has enormous potential. One tourist guidebook suggests it may prove Orkney to have been the cultural centre of Britain before Scotland, London, or almost everywhere else, had been invented! It proves how much there is yet to be discovered. Maybe it will inspire another book!

The Flotta Oil Terminal is real enough, and I use some of its statistics (from the web site). I have no idea how it is run, beyond what I found on the web site, I have invented that to suit the story. One might imagine that the story starts somewhere between 2003 - 2005

Nor should any conservation body take exception to *PPP* which is my invention (which is just as well!).

My thanks to Murdo Grant for considerable help and for the original phrase "I cannot eat more than six kippers for breakfast". As tutor to the Black Isle Writers club some years ago, it was an exercise in short story writing. Mine grew too long so I put it aside. At last I have been able to finish it!

Elizbeth Sutherland for encouragement and important suggestions, all of which have I am sure, made the story much better than it would have otherwise been.

Jane & Damian Robinson, archaeologists, York, for relevant advice.

Jimmy Fraser for advice on bail procedures and in other respects.

Dedication

To my wife Jane, who deserves the dedication of this book for tolerating me constantly disappearing into my study just when she wanted me to do something else!

The Overture

As he read an article in his newspaper about a new find in Shetland whilst waiting for his flight from Dalcross to be called, Ellis Mackenzie caught a phrase from the table behind him; "I can't eat more than six kippers for breakfast."

A curious private joke? Or had he misheard? He returned to his paper with a chuckle – it would have been rude to turn to look.

At 24 he was Archeological Surveyor for the North Region of Treasures of Scotland, a job which he felt lucky to hold. As a young archeologist it was both an excellent start to his career, and it was also in an area that he loved. He was based in Inverness.

Ellis especially enjoyed his trips to the Northern Isles. The folk he met and worked with were friendly, helpful and a pleasure to know. His current role included keeping a watching brief on how sites open to the public were standing up to the inevitable wear and tear from visitors, making recommendations for work required to ensure the monuments were well cared for, and assessing new finds. The task meant a couple of visits a year to each of Orkney and Shetland. This visit was to Orkney, and he was looking forward to it.

However enjoyable these working trips, the planes used for the Inverness to Kirkwall route were noisy, cramped and not very comfortable. Once on board reading a newspaper was not really possible, so when airborne and with another coffee, he turned to his neighbour and, for something to say asked, "Do you use this uncomfortable plane much?"

"No, it is the first and hopefully the last time. I do not like flying, but I am late."

"I think the journey well worth the discomfort," said Ellis, "this is my third visit, and I always enjoy it. It always seems an adventure, something always happens."

Ellis studied the clouds for a while, then, as his neighbour did not appear to share his enthusiasm, added "Even in the airport I heard the most curious thing. Someone said 'I cannot eat more than six kippers for breakfast'."

The man beside him seemed to tense, and grumpily replied "You should not listen to other people's conversations." The accent seemed to have a slight Irish inflection.

Ellis was saved from his mild embarrassment at this reproach, by the announcement that they were about to start their descent into Kirkwall airport, accompanied by the usual scurry to remove the coffee cups. But he wondered why his neighbour was quite so grumpy. He thought the incident was funny.

He turned to look out of the window to enjoy the view of Scapa Flow as they dropped below the clouds. He admired this wonderful expanse of water laid out like a map below. In the foreground he saw a small oil slick. Oddly there was a large green ketch in the middle of it. He saw the crew looking over the side as if they had some special interest in it. Silly yachties, he thought, they will just get a very dirty waterline doing that, and surely everyone knew it came from the wreck of the Royal Oak? Then the view changed to farmland which always interested Ellis, for archeological sites are often spotted from above. It was, of course, a vain thought, as the fields flashed by far too quickly for him to spot anything.

From previous visits he immediately recognized Vaila Flett, secretary in the Orkney office when he emerged from the delightfully small terminal. She had come to take him to the office. She was standing by the company car talking on her mobile.

He took his time walking over to her, to let her finish her call, and he was reminded of what an attractive girl she was; dark hair, nearly black, dark sparking eyes, and wearing an Orkney sweater and jeans in which she was obviously comfortable. A girl to turn any head, he thought. She saw him and waved, and putting the phone away shook his hand. , "Good flight, Mr. Mackenzie?" she asked. She thought he looked like the archeologist he was, in sports jacket and dark trousers, which seemed rather well worn. Just a little taller than herself, not bad looking too, especially when he smiled, but not, she thought, a sporty type.

"Yes, but a very curious thing happened. Do you see the man by the green car over there talking to another man with a beard? He was the one who turned a strange and funny remark into a mystery. I'll tell you in the car."

"I think they are talking about you; they keep glancing this way. Anyway, let's go, Magnus seems to be in a hurry."

On the way into Kirkwall Ellis said "Can I call you Vaila?"

"We are not formal here! I am Vaila to everyone. It's a Shetland name really, but no one minds."

"Fine, then I'm Ellis." That agreed, he told her the story, ending by asking "Is six kippers some sort of Orcadian saying – and do you recognize those men?"

"No to both. The men are certainly not locals. I've never heard of anyone eating six kippers at one sitting either." She laughed "They would repeat on you for a week!"

As Vaila drove and he looked around he reflected once again on his good fortune to be actually paid to work at the things that most interested him, coupled with doing the work in such wonderful places. Orkney after all is an archeologist's heaven. He was also fascinated by the ways of judging and balancing the conservation of the sites with the provision of access to the public. It was a problem even on Orkney, where the number of visitors is far lower than in mainland Scotland, let alone England.

Magnus was the Orkney manager, a large man always smiling, so far as one could tell behind his luxuriant beard. Magnus and Vaila were the only regular full time staff in the office, which was tucked down a small vennel near the centre of Kirkwall. He greeted Ellis warmly, again asking if he had had a good journey.

Pleasantries over, Magnus asked Ellis what specific tasks he had on this trip.

"A miscellaneous list. The boss wants me to look at the new find on Bustahead Farm. It appears to be some sort of souterrean from the description. The farmer is, I gather from the boss, a bit reluctant to give us much access to it, but hopefully I can at least see it.

Then it has been suggested that some of the World War remains on Flotta should be stabilized or even restored. I gather that there is also a proposal to extend the oil terminal, conveniently for me also on Flotta, so I am to check that there are no archeological sites affected. In my spare time, he says, I should speak to you about path erosion at some of the places which have larger numbers of visitors, such as Skara Brae. Could we perhaps have a look together? Maybe you also have some things you would like me to take up with the regional office, or even HQ if I dare."

"All that in a couple of days!" laughed Magnus "Well, why don't I take you to Scara Brae straight away; we can leave your bags at the hotel on the way if you like."

Having settled the programme they set off in the car, taking the Stromness road, discussing the various aspects of their work as they went.

Their conversation was interrupted by a flash of green as a car overtook them at great speed on the long straight near Maeshow. Ellis' view was filled for a split second by the car's passenger staring at him. It was over quickly, but Ellis had the impression that they were being inspected, as if someone was trying to discover who they were.

"What on earth was that all about?" said Magnus "Not a very Orcadian way to drive, and what was that passenger staring at?"

Ellis replied, "I am fairly sure that was the man who was so grumpy about my having heard a strange thing at Dalcross this morning" and he repeated the story about the six kippers. "Something of a mystery to me," He concluded. "I am not sure, but I think that was the same green car I saw at the airport where someone was picking up my grumpy fellow passenger. Vaila said that neither he nor the man he met were Orcadians."

"Well no one can keep a secret for long here" said Magnus with a chuckle, "I expect we will know all about it before long."

They soon reached Skara Brae where they met the custodian. First they walked out to the prehistoric village, once more it impressed Ellis as the most amazing 6000 year old survival of a complete Stone Age village, with the bonus of being in an attractive wide sandy bay. Watching the reaction of visitors, one of whom seemed vaguely familiar, he felt surprised that the site was not busier than it was. As a world heritage site, and unique in many ways, it is so well preserved that you could imagine living there. It was surely a 'must see' for anyone on holiday in northern Scotland, let alone those wanting to study ancient history.

They returned to the visitor centre and checked the interpretive boards. Over a sandwich lunch in the café Ellis asked Drew, the custodian, how the season was going.

"This visitor centre has made a lot of difference to both the monument and our visitors alike. It is true that visitors used to love being able to walk into the passages and into each dwelling, but numbers have grown so much that there was not only a risk of damage and wear and tear to the village, but because they also walked around at roof level, unguarded, health and safety was also an issue. Then, of course, there is the weather. We have to close the site in really strong winds, folk have been blown over! The reconstructed 'house' here in the centre is therefore especially appreciated, as it gives a reasonable idea of what life must have been like, so long as you forget it is made of plastic!"

"Mind you" added Magnus laughing" if we could find some way to make it smelly it would add to the authenticity!"

At that moment, Magnus' phone rang, and after a brief conversation. He switched off his phone and said "I must get back to Kirkwall."

Turning to Drew he asked "I think you said you were going into town this afternoon, could you give me a lift to the office?"

"No problem, we could leave at once if you like."

Magnus handed the office car keys to Ellis. "I'm afraid you'll have to look at the other sites by yourself. We 'll catch up later."

Ellis replied "How about dinner tonight at the hotel?"

"What, no pretty girl to keep you company?"

"Now, now what would your wife say if she knew you can't think of dinner without a pretty girl in attendance? I think you'd better bring Margaret with you to ensure you behave yourself! See you both at 7.30 then."

But in his mind's eye Ellis could not help thinking of Vaila, after all she was the only girl he knew in Orkney, and she was undeniably pretty.

As they started to leave through the shop, there was a crash behind them. Ellis spun round to see a small boy with an uncertain expression on his face and his mother red with embarrassment. Several folk, including Magnus and Ellis, moved to start picking up the goods that had fallen off the collapsed shelf. Magnus reassured the mother, "It's fine, nothing is breakable, the boy meant no harm and everything will soon be put right." With a charming smile, turned to go with Drew.

Ellis stood up to replace an item which had rolled under an adjacent book case, and found himself eyeball to eyeball with the man he had thought he recognized at the village, but he still could not remember where he had seen him before. The man said nothing, put the item he had picked up back on the shelf, smiled at Ellis and walked away, leaving Ellis none the wiser.

Ellis' next stop was at the Ring of Brodgar. He walked right round the circle, just as a visitor would, checking the path. By now the sun had come out and he was enjoying thinking more about the stones themselves than checking the path. Looking at their careful placing and the outlook to other landmarks. The shape of the land, the sea in the distance, and the sound of the wind walking with him as if it had a message for him, these were all part of the Ring. Day dreaming of what the message might be and of chants to ancient gods, and of life so long ago, Ellis wondered yet again just what it must have been like. What was this ring of stones really for, to have been worth so much time and effort to construct? Someone must have thought it was an important project. Was it perhaps the same desires, a similar motivation, that lead many generations later to the building of St Magnus Cathedral in Kirkwall? Part memorial, part worship of something beyond the world they could see, something deeply felt if not fully understood?

His revery was interrupted by a flash of light, a reflection of the sun on glass. It came from the direction of the stones of Stenness a couple miles to the south. Was someone looking at him through binoculars or had he too vivid an imagination?

Returning to the car, Ellis took out the binoculars kept in the locker to try to work out what had reflected the sun. He thought he knew where it came from, but could see nothing.

As he drove down to Stenness, he passed the area becoming known as the 'Ness of Brodgar'. He was a little cross with himself that in thinking about flashes of light, he hadn't even thought about the discussion going on between his seniors of the possibility of a new excavation between Brodgar and Stenness, until he had passed it. It sounded as if it would be a really important project. If that came off would he be coming north more often he wondered? He hoped so.

Next he went to Maeshow, and being by now late afternoon, he was only just in time to catch Mrs. Isbister as she was closing and locking the monument. He did not want to delay her so just introduced himself and had a brief chat about the visitor season.

"Oh it's been quite good this year, and it's not long started. I've had nearly fifty just this afternoon"

"Did you by any chance have a visit from one or two men in a green car?" Ellis asked.

"How would I know that?" she said, "I only meet folk when they have walked across to the monument, so I rarely know how they got here."

"Of course, silly of me and it doesn't matter. Incidentally do you get many visitors for the mid winter solstice – I'd love to see that myself."

Mrs. Isbister, habitually cheerful, but a realist, replied "Then bring the sun with you, it usually rains and blows a gale!"

"I wonder if the folk who built these places had that problem" Ellis said as he thanked her and left. As he pulled out of the car park, turning right to Kirkwall, he naturally glanced left to check the traffic. He saw in the distance a green car. It appeared to be stationary and unoccupied in a layby.

During the drive back to Kirkwall he mused on the day. Was it his imagination that someone was checking on his movements, but if not, why were there so many occasions when he saw half familiar faces, some of them apparently interested in him? Why did he keep seeing green cars, when it was not, he thought a very popular colour? Certainly the car he drove had Treasures of Scotland written on it, so anyone who wanted to know where he went could not have found it hard to find out.

'Don't be silly,' he told himself, 'you'll think you're James Bond next. Just concentrate on why you are here.'

It was around four thirty when Ellis drove into the garage in which the office car was kept. He went to the office to leave the car keys and found Vaila by herself getting ready to go home.

She said "Hello. Magnus asked me to tell you that he's gone home early as he has to meet a builder who was doing some repairs to his house. He said he'd see you later for dinner as arranged."

"Fine. Have you had a good day, Vaila?"

"All routine, except for a man with a foreign accent asking if we had an archeologist. I told him that we only had a visiting archeologist, but that he was out at various sites today. He did not say why he wanted to know."

"I had the feeling that someone was following me around. Which sort of reminds me, do you have a file about the new finds at Ness of Brodgar?"

Yes, I'll get it for you." She took it out of the cabinet and gave it to him.

"Thank you. I'd like to borrow this for tomorrow, as I ought to know more about the site. It sounds most interesting and certainly significant. Remind me to return it before I fly home."

He leafed through some of the papers in the file and then closed it. "Maybe I'll read it as I dine tomorrow night, seeing my Mum will not be there to tell me off for reading at the table! She's right of course, and it would be much more fun to have company. You wouldn't happen to be free to have dinner with me tomorrow evening by any chance?"

"I did not enjoy my last date, so I'm off men just now, and I have lots other things to do, so thank you, but no thank you. Anyway you couldn't justify charging a meal with me to expenses, as doubtless you can dining with Magnus."

"Oh dear I seem to be in the dog house along with your last host! Reluctantly I'll accept your 'no' but it's a bit hard to accuse me of fiddling my expenses." He tapped the file "But could it become a working dinner if I correct your spelling of 'archeologist'?"

She scowled at him and he smiled back until she realized he was teasing her.

"My last date would not have hesitated to charge the cost of a dinner with me to expenses."

"The invitation was from me, Vaila, not Treasurers of Scotland and it's still open should you change your mind. Sorry to tease, it isn't an easy word to spell."

"My apologies too, Ellis, for being rude, but I just do not want to go on another date just now."

"Apology accepted, maybe on my next visit. Meanwhile I will return to my lonely hotel room. Good evening, Vaila. See you tomorrow, no doubt."

At 7.30 exactly, Magnus and his wife Margaret walked into the Kirkwall Hotel. Ellis had only met Margaret once before, briefly, but as they walked towards him he thought they looked well matched. Magnus' great beard and ready smile was matched by her happy expression as she greeted several folk in the bar whom she knew. It reminded Ellis that everyone knew everyone here, or so it seemed.

During dinner Magnus and Ellis inevitably talked about Ellis' visit and their work, until Margaret insisted they changed the subject.

She spoke to Ellis "The St Magnus Festival takes place here in a few weeks' time, and I am in the choir. Vaila's Mum is also in it. I am especially keen on two concerts in which we have a part, one singing the Mozart Requiem – sad but beautiful is my verdict. The other is a Bach programme and some of the pieces will be accompanied by the relevant original instruments."

"I've not heard the music played that way before." Ellis thought how much he would like to hear it, but work would doubtless prevent him from doing so this time.

As they had coffee, Magnus said "That underground chamber you want to visit tomorrow on Bustahead Farm may present the problems the boss mentioned, as James Anderson, the farmer there, is very suspicious of us. I think he believes the world and his wife will trample all over his land if he lets anyone near it. You are from Inverness which makes it worse. Why don't you take Vaila with you to smooth your negotiations? Anderson is a relation of Hal and Vaila's family."

Ellis was delighted with this idea, but asked "Is Hal Vaila's brother?"

"Oh I forgot you have not met him – yes, he is. They are very close as brother and sister."

"Can you spare her from the office?"

"Of course he can," replied Margaret, with a grin before Magnus could reply. "It will be another day my husband is spared temptation."

Magnus roared with laughter. "No, Margaret you know I love only you!"

"Yes dear," she said and turning to Ellis added "Magnus knows how his bread is buttered."

So it was arranged that Ellis would call in the office first thing in the morning to complete the day's arrangements.

Saying a cheerful good night and thanking Ellis for dinner, Margaret and Magnus left, and Ellis turned in.

Underground

When Ellis sat down to breakfast the next morning he was thinking of the day and especially how to approach the farmer on whose land the underground chamber had been discovered. If both his boss and Magnus thought he might have to overcome some reluctance even to allow him to explore it, then he must take the problem seriously. He hoped he could get Mr. Anderson's consent because, from the description he had been given, it appeared to be similar, if smaller, than Minehowe at Tankerness. No one was sure what Minehowe was, so it seemed possible that this new find might offer clues to both structures. If so he might have an especially interesting day. Whilst the archeology was meat and drink to him, he did not feel comfortable negotiating access, not least because he had sympathy with a working farmer not wanting his farming operations messed up by archeological folk like himself, or worse being invaded by a public keen to see the latest find. He could not reassure Mr. Anderson about anything until he had seen it; a bit like 'Heads he wins and tails I lose'. He could only hope that Vaila's presence would solve the problem.

Thinking about this task he was not concentrating on choosing his meal, so was slightly off guard when the waiter appeared beside him asking for his order. Without thinking he said "Certainly not more than six kippers"

"You must not say that here," said the waiter in a cross semi whisper, with a distinctly foreign accent.

"Why does everyone react when I say things about kippers?" replied Ellis and seeing the startled expression on the waiters face continued, "Oh I'll just have bacon and egg, brown toast and coffee, please."

What is this about kippers? He thought, it is getting irritating. Why should a waiter with a Polish, or at least eastern European, accent get upset about the six kippers? Vaila had said that the man who had gone into the office asking about archeologists had a foreign accent, could it have been the waiter?

To make it worse when he left the dining room he saw the waiter talking to a man who looked like the one who had followed him around Scara Brae. He did not want them to see him looking at them, so he was unable to be sure. Both seemed quite young and had a sallow complexion which might suggest both were Eastern European. Why were they so interested in the kippers he wondered again?

Ellis walked to the office, where he found Vaila dealing with the post. "Good morning Vaila. Has Magnus spoken to you about today?" he asked.

"He's not in yet. What's the idea then?"

"My first job today is to go to Bustahead farm and see if Mr. Anderson will allow me to inspect the underground structure he has found. Both my boss and Magnus thought he might be reluctant, but Magnus told me he is a relation of your family and at dinner last night suggested I ask you to come with me. Would you like to do that?"

"Anything for a day out, yes of course. Our cousin is in fact quite interested in the thing he found, it's just that he doesn't want folk poking around and upsetting his stock. Did Magnus know that my brother Hal is also working there today?"

"No, that's wonderful, although it is a pity I have not met Hal before or I would have two of you to reassure him that I am not that bad a character. Anyway, I'm ready when you are."

"Can I first deal with the post?"

"Is it fascinating today?"

"No, why does HQ keep sending statistics of places in Galloway? What use can we make of those?"

At that moment Magnus arrived, greeted them both and said to Vaila in a stage whisper, "Is this man luring you away from me? Oh how I suffer!" he laughed.

"Yes I think it would help Ellis, if you could give James Anderson reassurance that Ellis is quite civilized, even if he does come from Inverness! Take the office car" Turning to Ellis he added "You will find a folding ladder, a hard hat and a torch in the boot to help your inspection assuming you intend going down into it."

"Oh yes, thank you. The boss said you had everything I would need. I must look at it properly and get some photos. Inevitably I am expected to write a report."

Vaila said to Magnus, "These few letters may be of interest, the rest is routine stuff from HQ. If you dictate replies on the dictaphone I can type them when we get back."

"Fine, off you go then and be good – and careful. I've never enjoyed these underground places myself. Perhaps I am just too big for them." And he roared with laughter.

Vaila smiled and said "We can go now Ellis"

"What do you know about this find?" Ellis asked Vaila, as they drove out of Kirkwall.

"Nothing much. My cousin says it appears to be a simple round hole in the ground about one and a half metres across and perhaps five metres deep lined with stone. It withstood his tractor going over it a month ago but the covering slab was dislodged and that's how it was found. We are hoping you can tell us what it is."

When they drove into the steading Ellis saw two men talking together. One, Ellis thought, looked every inch a farmer. An outdoors face, with a cheerful, if watchful, expression above a strong body. The younger man had a cheerful smile, and was easily identified as Vaila's brother; the family resemblance was obvious.

The farmer greeted Vaila warmly. "Hello Vaila, always a delight to see you. Who is this you've brought with you?"

"Hello, James, this is Ellis Mackenzie, our archeologist from Inverness. It was for him I made the appointment. He would like to have a look at the hole in the ground you told us about."

Turning to Ellis she said, "Meet my cousin James Anderson, and this is my self-appointed protector, big brother Hal. He mends things for a living. He's very pleased with himself because he has just got a part time job as maintenance surveyor at the Flotta oil terminal – just for the non-oil buildings of course." Ellis immediately liked Hal. He had the sort of face that looked as if it was used to smiling.

"Congratulations. That sounds interesting. I have to go to Flotta tomorrow so I must ask you about it."

Turning to Mr. Anderson, "Good to meet you. It is very kind of you to let me see your find, Mr. Anderson." He wondered if he was being presumptuous of approval, but it had worked for him before.

"Oh ay, well, just before you have a look at it, you should know that I dinn'a want hordes of folk poking around the farm disturbing the stock and all that. So is it just you looking? Or will you be followed by a muckle crowd of students digging away as they are doing elsewhere? And I'm even less keen on any public showing. I'd never get the work done for them asking daft questions. That would be worse still."

"To be honest," said Ellis, "I am only a junior archaeologist and so do not get to make such decisions, but I suggest I have a look first. There may be nothing for you to worry about. It is not just a case of the importance of your hole in the ground but also of the practical side. Is it unusual, is it worth looking further, is it safe enough to allow the public near it and so on. So if it is okay by you I'll have a look and then we can talk about it afterwards. I will have to write a report for my boss of course, but you are welcome to read it."

"Very well. I presume you have a ladder and so on in the car, and as the ground is hard enough, why don't you take the car to the site?"

Thanking him, Ellis asked if Hal had the time to come too, as he thought he might need help especially getting into, and out of the hole.

"So long as the repairs to my machinery get done this morning," replied Mr. Anderson before Hal could say anything. "So I'll look forward to hearing what you make of it later. I'll be in the yard, I dare say."

Hal got into the back of the car, and Vaila drove across the field behind the steading and stopped the car a few yards from the hole, which had been marked by a large fence post, but was otherwise not protected. The three of them peered into it from above, and Ellis noted that it was indeed roughly the size Vaila had told him and the stone work appeared solid enough, so he fetched the ladder and, unfolding it, lowered it into the hole. It was only just long enough but was firm, so putting on the hard hat, and carrying the torch on a lanyard round his neck Ellis climbed down the ladder.

He looked carefully at the stone work as he went down and was glad to see it was in good condition even after the thousands of years since it was built. In fact it had the neatness of the stonework inside Maeshowe, rather than the more random build of Minehowe. When he reached the bottom, he noted the floor of this chamber was also stone, so there was no risk of the ladder sinking in.

"What can you see?" asked Vaila from above.

"What is it, what's it for?" asked Hal.

"I do not think it is a tomb – wrong shape," replied Ellis. "Nor was it a well, for the same reason, and anyway it is dry now and shows no sign of ever having had water in it. It might have been for storage maybe of winter food supplies. They would remain cool down here. It seems unremarkable – oh what's this? Hang on." He bent down shining the torch on the wall at about a knee height. "There is a small passage or tunnel on this side. That's surprising, I wasn't expecting that, although in all fairness that makes it more like Minehowe which has several such passages."

Getting down on his haunches he peered into the passage with the help of the torch. The passage seemed to be a little under two metres long and from the little he could see, there was a space beyond. Perhaps, he thought, another small chamber. He tried to get into the passage. Try as he might it was just too small for him.

Ellis stood up and called to the two of them above him, "There is a small passage which appears to lead to another small chamber. I cannot quite get into it to see what is there. My shoulders are too wide. My camera is in the car. Could you hand it down and I'll see if I can at least get a photo by reaching in as far as I can."

With the camera, Ellis took some photos of the first chamber, and of the passage. Then he stretched into the passage as far as he could, one handed. He took two or three flash pictures, but when he looked at them on the camera's screen it told him nothing. He called up, "It's no good we will just have to accept that it is too small a passage to get through until we can find a very small person to crawl in – or more likely a selfie stick!"

He bent down to look again, and as he did so he heard Hal say "Oh no you can't Vaila, don't be silly."

Ellis stood up to find Vaila beside him, "Let me try I am smaller than you."

"No Vaila, we have no idea what is there, or even how stable the passage is, let alone the chamber beyond. It's not worth the risk."

"Why do men always think girls aren't up to things like this Ellis? You tried, so why not me? I want to have a go. I shall, like Star Trek, be the girl to boldly go into the unknown. I think I can get in there. So why not?"

"Well I really do not like the idea but if you insist you should at least wear the hard hat. Adjust it to fit firmly ensuring the chin strap is reasonably tight so it cannot be dislodged. I will shine the torch because when you are right in you will not be able to hold it as well as the camera.

Vaila looked at the passage carefully and tried tentatively to get in. She said "I think I need to go in with my arms ahead of me – over my head. That should work." She climbed into the passage wriggling and pushing herself in by her elbows and knees.

She called "I can get hold of the floor where it drops into this chamber but you may need to pull me back as there is only a little space beside me."

"What's happening?" called Hal.

"She has got into the passage, but it's a tight fit, and she has only a little spare space between the wall and herself."

Vaila said "I have taken some photos looking down but I'll have to try to turn over to see how high the chamber is."

There was a thud. A sound of falling earth, and Vaila's startled "Oh! "

Ellis' heart missed a beat. Shining the torch into the passage he could see what had happened. In trying to turn over Vaila had caught a stone that had been supporting the lintel of the second chamber so that it had dropped. It appeared to be resting on the hard hat.

"Can you move Vaila?"

"No, for some reason I cannot move my head. I'm stuck and I can't see a thing. I cannot even get rid of the earth on my face, on everywhere, and because my arms are in the chamber, I cannot withdraw them into the tunnel, it's too small."

"We'll soon get you out, Vaila," said Ellis, whilst wondering if they could.

The lintel looked a large and heavy stone and he didn't think it would be easy to dislodge it. "Try to keep still. There is a stone wedged across the hard hat. With your arms trapped above your head, I doubt if you can undo the hat to leave it there and even if you could I think it would be risky. I cannot reach it either as you fill all the space. I am going to have a word with Hal and we will, I promise, get you out as soon as we can."

He stood up again and explained the situation to Hal. "Have we a jack in the car with which I could lift the stone that is trapping Vaila?

"I'll see" and Hal returned to the car. He was back in a few moments with a small bottle jack which had a long handle to turn the screw.

"What about this?"

"I will try, it is small enough to get in place but I will have to be very careful it holds the stone properly. Hand it and the handle down."

When he had it he looked again into the passage with the torch to decide exactly where to place it.

"Vaila, Hal has got me a small jack so I am now going to get it down your left side and under the stone that is trapping you. The idea is to lift the stone enough to free you, but it will be a bit tricky to get it in a position where the stone will be properly balanced on the jack. I think I will need to push it in with the handle, and that means it might go hard into your left side. I will try not to hurt you but I have to get it right under the stone. Tell me if it hurts, but even if it does, can you try to keep very still? I will try to be quick and I'll explain what I am doing as I work. The main thing is to ensure it is in the right place."

"I will do my best. Is this hat really strong enough? It seems to be squashing a bit, as I can feel it on my head."

"Oh yes, I'm sure it is, this is what it is designed for." But he wondered. The truth was he really had no idea.

He put the jack in as far as he could reach, about level with her waist with the long handle attached.

"Now I must push," he said. "If I can get the jack a little way beyond your armpit, roughly where your shoulder would be if your arms were at your side that may be far enough as it is a wide stone. As you are right up against the side I'll have to force it up as I told you just now. At least the jack cannot fall over."

The last few centimetres were especially difficult for him, and he feared it must be painful for Vaila, but he knew it was the only way, and she never made a sound or moved a muscle. Even then he was scared of the stone moving so as to fall on Vaila herself. He felt a moment of real fear; what if it fell across her neck? He blanked out the thought by concentrating on what he was doing.

Carefully inspecting the position of the jack again with the torch, he said "Vaila, the jack is where I think it will lift the stone enough to free you. I hope you'll feel the pressure coming off you, but remain as still as you can, as we do not want to disturb anything else. I will pull you out when I think the stone is high enough. Here we go." The latter said as confidently as he could. Not true of course, he was not at all confident it would work.

31

He slowly turned the handle to raise the jack. Very slowly he felt it grip the stone and lift it. One millimeter, two, three. With the torch he thought he could see space between the stone and the hat.

"The stone has just lifted a fraction off the hat, Vaila, so I'm going to pull you from the knees to see if I can free you. Please do not try to move, just remain limp. Leave the pulling to me. Think of the celebration when you are out."

Hoping he still sounded confident to her, he reached in once more and, holding her legs under her knees, gently pulled. To his enormous relief he felt her move, so he pulled a bit harder, and smoothly pulled her right out of the passage. He then lifted her from the ground so she was standing. "Are you Okay on your feet?"

"A bit wobbly but so relieved to be out of there. I was so scared in that horrid passage," and she fell against him, hugging him for comfort and shivering with relief, her head on his shoulder.

"Is all well?" called Hal from above.

"Yes, she's out and fine, just needing a moment to recover."

"Well done you two" said Hall, "come right up when you are ready."

He held her, being careful of her left side not being sure if she had been bruised by the jack. He removed the hard hat and stroked her hair, because he did not know what else to do that might help calm her. When she had recovered, she said, "Thank you Ellis, I am so relieved that you were there to pull me out. I think I'm OK now. Can you just give me a hand up the ladder?"

Once in the open air Hal embraced her. "When you're ready piddie sister, I'll take you home."

Ellis, who had by now retrieved the jack at the cost of blocking the passage altogether, climbed out. "One benefit, I suppose, for the tunnel collapsing is that it is likely to prove difficult or impossible to explore it further. That may be reassuring for Mr. Anderson even if only temporarily."

Ellis continued "Unfortunately I am no nearer working out what this structure is, or was for. Pity really as the second chamber is, I think, most unusual. I'm not sure what to make of it. I'll have a better look at the photos when I get back to my office.

"If you are taking Vaila home, in your own car, Hal, I will tell Mr. Anderson what I found and then return to the office – oh and one more thing; I would prefer we say no more about this incident beyond the family, and I suppose Magnus. I don't want health and safety breathing down my neck."

"That's fine and please apologize to James for me. Tell him I'll be back in the morning to finish the repairs. He may grumble, but he has a soft spot for Vaila so I do not think he will be too upset."

When he got back to the office, Ellis told Magnus that he had been down the hole, that there was a small passage, which lead to a second equally empty chamber. The passage was too small for him, and he explained that Vaila had been determined to see if she could get into it.   Anyway she did not find anything interesting and then got stuck, so I had to pull her out. Consequently Hal has taken her home as she ended up covered in earth.

"That girl is a feisty soul. One day she might get in a jam she can't get out of, but you have to admit she has spirit!" Ellis smiled and thought that Magnus was all too right. But if anything serious had happened to her what on earth would he have done? He shivered at the thought.

At that moment the phone rang. A rather puzzled Magnus said, "It's Vaila's Mum. Now you're in trouble!"

Ellis shrugged his shoulders, and took the phone. "Hello, Ellis MacKenzie here" After a long gap he said "Yes, well it is very kind of you to say so, but I should be apologizing for allowing her to get stuck in the first place." Magnus heard another longish silence, then "Thank you very much, I'd love to, I wanted to call anyway to ensure she was fully recovered. At 7.30 then, I'll look forward to meeting you."

He turned to Magnus, "That was Vaila's mum. She was thanking me for getting Vaila out, though I am not at all sure I deserve her thanks. I just wish I had stopped her going into the tunnel. Anyway they have kindly asked me to dinner tonight."

Magnus grinned. "Knowing Vaila I doubt if you could have stopped her. Let me also caution you my good friend, when the mother takes an interest in you, you had better watch out, the matchmaker is about!" He laughed.

"You're a rotten tease," replied Ellis, "but I don't think I am in much danger."

The phone rang a second time. Ellis, right beside it, picked it up to find that this time it was Hal. "Just ringing to ask if you knew that there is an exhibition in the Town Hall about plans to expand the oil terminal on Flotta, followed by a meeting about 5pm this afternoon. Vaila says you spoke

34

about checking on their plans, as well as looking at some of the World War remains there, so would you like to come with me to see what it is all about?"

"Thanks. That's right, I have to check that the expansion will not affect any known archeology anyway, so if there is an exhibition it might save some time."

Pause.

"Thank you, yes, your Mum told me, thank goodness she's OK, we had some anxious moments there." After a moment or two, "You mean she wants to come too? She must be OK. You have a feisty sister alright. I must go to the hotel and have a good wash after being down in the chamber. I'll meet you at the hall in about thirty minutes. Great, I'll see you both at the hall. Good bye"

He turned to Magnus. "Hal says Vaila's fine, unhurt and fully recovered from her adventure. Also there is a meeting and exhibition about future plans for the terminal on Flotta, and as I had planned on going there tomorrow, and need to be back in time for the afternoon flight home, the exhibition might save me some time. Vaila thinks she needs to get out, and asks if she can come too. I'm afraid you are not going to get your typing done to day."

"Oh how I suffer! Don't worry about it there's not much typing today and the other tasks can wait too. I'm just relieved to hear Vaila is fully recovered and she'll surely be fine with the two of you to look after her."

THE MEETING

Ellis walked into the hall and looked around. He could not see Hal and Vaila so he crossed the room to look at a detailed plan of Flotta set on a pair of very large display screens, placed across a corner alcove from which a band might normally play. He noted from the plan where the ferry pier was and that the wartime buildings were on the Golta peninsular, a long thin finger of land running eastward with Roan Head at the end of it. Included on the plan were the sites of the YMCA, the rocket battery and the St Vincent Pier, but without any indication of exactly what remained of them.

The oil terminal covered a large area, so large that the road to Golta went through part of it, which explained the need for the permit which his office had already obtained for him. The sites of the World War buildings were about two miles from the ferry pier. The position of the proposed expansion was shown, and appeared well clear of any archaeology.

He decided that he could take the ferry and ideally could walk to the sites, and so long as the weather held it should give him some exercise. He would need to ensure he could get to the airport for the late afternoon flight home, so he would have to be certain that he could get to the sites and back in the time available. He found himself hoping that Vaila would drive him to the airport, although he supposed that by now Magnus would be thinking she should do the work waiting for her in the office and he would have to take a taxi.

Looking at the plan, and thinking of next day's arrangements, he was hardly aware of a discussion taking place in the alcove behind the screens. The screens were so solid and large that he could not see round or even under them, but he could hear the discussion clearly although he took little interest until someone mentioned six kippers. Then he started listening intently. There appeared to be three men involved, and he recognized two of the voices. The man who had told him not to listen to other people's conversations on the plane – Grumpy he had christened him - seemed to be leading the discussion. Ellis briefly thought it funny that he was now listening again to Grumpy's conversation. The second man was, he thought, the waiter in his hotel, with his distinctive East European accent. But he did not recognize the third voice. So acting as if studying the map and taking notes from it, he was able to make brief notes of what he heard.

Ten minutes passed before he heard Grumpy say "OK, that's enough for now, especially as you are on to gossip now. Disperse, go into the room separately listen and watch, but whatever the speakers say even if you do not like it, keep quiet. We should not draw attention to ourselves. Good luck."

Ellis moved smartly away from the screens, so was on the far side of the room when the first man appeared from behind them. At the same moment Hal and Vaila arrived at the door and waved, so he was able to go over to them as if he had not been anywhere near the board.

Quietly he said to them, "I must tell you what I have just heard, where can I do so in private?"

Vaila, seeing he was serious, said, "The room where actors and so on can get ready for plays. No one will be there at the moment. Come with me."

When they were seated and sure it was safe to talk Ellis told them what he had just overheard.

"When I came into the hall and realised you two had not yet arrived I went to look at the large map of Flotta on the screens at the far end of the hall. While I was looking at it I heard a discussion going on between three men in the alcove behind the screens. I told you about the incident on the plane yesterday with the man I now call Grumpy. He seemed to be the leader. This morning at breakfast when the waiter asked for my order I said, without thinking, that I could not eat more than six kippers. It upset the waiter no end and he told me not to talk about the kippers like that. He was the second man also judging by his voice which is certainly not British. I did not recognise the third voice, but Grumpy called him Bill."

"What were they doing?" asked Hal.

"The three were talking about arrangements to do something at the Flotta terminal that would upset the management and would 'help the cause they are here to support' So Grumpy said. The implication was that the three – we could call them the plotters – were working for someone Grumpy called 'the boss'.

Vaila said, "Who is the boss? Did they give him a name?"

"No, he gave no clue who the boss was, perhaps because the other two already knew.

The boss had emphasized to Grumpy the need to ensure no oil was spilt, and said it was not in their interest to have anyone hurt. Unfortunately I did not pick up any clue as to what they actually intended to do either, but it clearly needed preparation and, apparently, three men, as Grumpy described it, in the front line. Grumpy asked Bill at this point when Sid would be joining them, and Bill told him that he was due next week. I presume this means the three were Grumpy, Bill and Sid. A yacht comes into it, which must be a big one as Grumpy said it would be their base. It's apparently called *Gaia Marina*. From what little Grumpy said about it, it suggested to me that it could be the large green ketch one I first saw from the air. Grumpy explained that it would have to go to fetch some equipment, but again I did not hear anything to suggest what that was."

"Is that all? It leaves me with all sorts of questions." Hal looked puzzled.

"Yes it was a tantalising conversation for me too. Something is going on but what?

The next bit was quite funny. They talked about me, much to my amusement! It was the waiter who asked Grumpy about the man who knew their password and even quoted it on several occasions. The waiter told the others he had checked the hotel register and knew my name, that I was an archaeologist and that I worked for Treasures of Scotland. He said he had been to their office yesterday and the girl there said they had a visiting archaeologist inspecting various sites."

"That's right, it all fits with the enquiry I told you about yesterday."

"I remember, Vaila. Grumpy said he thought it must be the same man who he had met on the flight in. Grumpy, the waiter, and a friend of his had discreetly, (so they thought) followed my movements yesterday and decided I was a genuine archaeologist. The visit to the office clearly was to be sure of it.

"Although they still worried about me knowing the password, Grumpy told the others that since they were now together there would no longer be a need to use the password. He explained how I had overheard the password at Dalcross when he had met the boss for instructions prior to flying to Orkney. Grumpy said he felt I was harmless. But one of them, possibly Bill, was still concerned that they had not discovered where I had been this morning. It was suggested that they looked out for me, but Grumpy thought I did not matter – they had better things to do he said.

"He then spoke of a local contact on Orkney – Grumpy just called him S. It seemed that the waiter, was their contact with S. He thought that while S was naturally interested in the money, he was also motivated by revenge. It made him ready to do anything to help.

"Apparently the waiter had taken S out for a drink, and after a few glasses of Highland Park, which I gather is the local malt whisky, S had told him that he was keen to help because he wanted to get back at both the company and some sod that they gave the maintenance job to, when it should have been given to him. Not only that, but, he said that bastard has a sister who S called the 'Ice Maiden'. She had been his girlfriend until she had missed her chance of a good time by turning on him in public. Apparently when he had kissed her at a dance, she had kneed him in a painful place, without warning. He didn't even know why. As it was in full view of everyone there S, the waiter reported, clearly found the insult worse than the pain, and that was why he wanted revenge.

"Whilst they thought this story hilarious, Grumpy said they should be careful, an angry man could be a danger to their plans, but S had the inside knowledge they required and the boss had told them to work with him. Apparently Grumpy had had the impression from the boss that S might be taken on as his assistant. Anyway no one had told S yet what they intended to do, so Grumpy thought they were in no danger of S leaking their plans."

Hal said "It sounds as if S could be Simon Smith, which means the sod is me, and his sister, the Ice Maiden, is Vaila. I certainly got the job which he wanted."

"I did go out with Simon for a short while. I thought I quite liked him at first. He is certainly good looking, and he treated me courteously to start with, he could be good company, and quite interesting when he tried. But he had wandering hands, and it slowly dawned on me that he just wanted me to go to bed with him, and I didn't like that. I am afraid I did hurt him with my knee at a dance as you heard. I have refused to go out with him since the dance but he still tries to persuade me. He won't take no for an answer. It's as if he won't accept that any girl could refuse him. Yes, and he does call me the Ice Maiden too, even to my face when I refuse him."

Ellis smiled, "If that's what you do when kissed, I must remember not to kiss you!"

"That's not funny, Ellis, it was horrible, he wouldn't stop groping me. When I told him to stop he just got worse – all in public too. He actually told me that if I relaxed I would enjoy it, which infuriated me. I couldn't stand it, I was embarrassed, and felt everyone would see, and think me a real tart. He held me so tightly I couldn't escape and that dance seemed as if it would to go on for ever.

"I remembered girls talking about using your knee to make a point, but I think I did it too hard. It certainly stopped him, and must have restored my reputation, but it hurt him more than I intended. Luckily Hal and Inga were there or goodness knows what he would have done if I had had to go home with him."

Ellis apologised for his tactlessness "Forgive me?"

Vaila replied "Maybe."

Ellis resumed his tale.

"Assuming S is who you think he is, and you are the 'Sod', Hal, he intends to ensure you get the blame for whatever they are going to do. How, he did not say. The contact said the thought gave S great pleasure.

"His plan for revenge on you, Vaila, assuming you are the 'Ice Maiden', was to dump you for Inga; do I presume that is the same girl you mentioned just now?"

"Now he is being silly" said Vaila, "He forgets she is not only Hal's girlfriend but my best friend too. Does he imagine I haven't told her what he does already? And she saw what happened at the dance. Ha! Some arrogant men have a ridiculously high opinion of themselves!"

Hal added," I must tell Inga, it will give her a good laugh!"

"In the meantime we had better go back to the hall." said Ellis.

They were just in time to hear the announcement that Mr Fergus, Public Relations Officer for the company, would explain the company's proposals for Flotta.

On the whole, the audience seemed satisfied with Fergus' presentation. There were questions about how many of the new jobs would go to Orcadians. Only one lady spoke against the expansion, largely because she thought the risk of an oil spill in Scapa Flow would be greatly increased. She got a reassurance from Fergus, and although she did not look as if she was entirely happy with it no one said anything in her support.

They noticed one of the plotters, as they now called them, listening intently and making notes. But he was just one in a crowd keeping himself to himself.

When it was over, Ellis saw a very smart young man stand up to go, then hesitate as he saw Hal and Vaila, apparently for the first time, and he came over. He was well dressed, with longish, carefully cut, blond hair and what might be thought to be film star looks.

"How nice to see you two, my friend Hal and his lovely sister. Vaila that is such an attractive sweater, the colour matches your eyes. I do believe you are more beautiful every time I see you." Vaila did not look impressed, so Simon turned to Hal, "I don't think I have congratulated you on getting the Maintenance Surveyor's post. They watch you carefully at the terminal so I hope you make a good job of it. I have decided to take up a more lucrative post elsewhere. Now you have that job and I start mine shortly, perhaps our paths will not cross so often. Maybe that will persuade you that you need not guard your lovely sister quite so closely, and I will get the chance to persuade her to think of me fondly again. After all I would have thought you both would be encouraging – everyone else seems to think I am a good catch for a girl."

"Thank you Simon and congratulations to you too for getting a new job. As for Vaila, although I would of course protect her if she needed it, you have personal experience that should have taught you she can look after herself!"

"Yes. I must take the blame for that. I went too fast for you Vaila. But if I am truly sorry, can we forgive and forget? Can we try again? Please believe me when I say that I still love you. If I promised not to touch you, would you come out to dinner with me soon?"

"You do talk rubbish and I do not think it is a good idea for me to go out with you again Simon. I prefer to remain your favourite Ice Maiden, keeping her distance, where she can do you no harm."

A slight nod of the head and he replied "But even an octopus might hope to remain friends? – Isn't that what you call me sometimes?"

43

"You know I do and why." Vaila replied this time with a smile "I expect we both think we have invented appropriate nick names for each other."

Taking notice of Ellis, Simon asked Vaila "To change the subject, are you not going to introduce me, Vaila? A new boyfriend perhaps - don't tell me I now have a rival for your affections?" Ellis wondered if he was joking, although he did not sound as if he thought it funny.

Vaila smiled "Ellis may I introduce you to my ex-boyfriend, (she emphasized the ex) Simon Smith. Simon meet Treasures of Scotland's archaeologist, Ellis MacKenzie."

"Delighted to meet you" said Simon, with a smile, "Orkney is a great playground for archaeologists." Looking at his jacket he continued "I should have guessed your profession, you look all ready to start a dig I see. There is a story that archaeologists are only interested in older girls – the older they get the more interested they are. But I suppose you have heard that one before, none the less if true it gives me comfort that you will not be a rival after all. You will just have heard that I blotted my copybook with her, though I meant no harm. Maybe you can help me persuade her to forgive me and trust me again? I live in hope of changing her mind." He shook hands, and added "I dare say someone like you will have plenty of girlfriends anyway so I need not worry!"

Smiling, Ellis replied "I have indeed heard that story a few times, most archaeologists have. Amusing as it may be, we take an interest in people of all ages and generations, good bad and indifferent, people are people and everything we know of folk from the past suggests they were not that different from ourselves. I'm sorry my being with Vaila and Hal troubles you. Vaila is a colleague with Treasures of Scotland and a friend. She seems to me to be quite able to make her own decisions, and anyway it is hardly for me to try to advise her with whom she goes out. For what it matters to you I have many friends at home, but do not call any of them girlfriends just now. I hope that does not worry you?"

"I am so sorry to hear you have no one special. Perhaps you should try a little harder. I could give you some tips maybe to help your social skills." He smiled, "But I suggest you avoid Vaila. She is as cold as your 6000 year olds, truly an ice maiden. I gave her every chance, offered all sorts of things, and even apologised for anything I have done she did not like, as you just heard, but with no sign of a thaw – yet. But I have not given up hope, because I really am very fond of her."

"Are you encouraging me to rise to the challenge, or warning me off territory you claim is yours, ice maiden or not? I must remember to ask Vaila which she would prefer."

Vaila laughed and Ellis continued "Most interesting to meet you, Simon, but I daresay you have many friends to speak to, and we are all having dinner together."

"All of you? Can't you take her out without big brother watching? You do need to improve your skills in these things. You are a rotten spoil sport Hal, but on second thoughts perhaps it is in my interests that you go together, as they say there is safety in numbers, in this case for me too. Hal, I am wondering if Inga will get tired of your spending so much time on baby sister. Cheerio. You'll be sorry we didn't make up Vaila – and you Hal will too – at least as much. Now while Vaila decides on Ellis' question, perhaps I'll ask Inga if she would like an interesting evening with me. That would be nice." He then moved away.

Ellis turned to Vaila and Hal, "What a slimy toad. Well done Vaila for seeing him off. I wish I had been there to see it! Now, what will your folk expect me to wear – I haven't any posh clothes with me but I could run to a clean shirt and tie?"

"You should come as you are –change your shirt if you like, but no tie needed." said Vaila.

Hal said "Fine. Then if we walk back to our house via the hotel, perhaps there would be time to think what we should do with what we have learnt this afternoon?"

After talking about it for a while they still remained undecided on what action to take. There seemed little point going to the police; no crime had been committed, and none of the three men behind the screen suggested that they had something illegal in mind. It might just be a demonstration, and neither the company, nor the police would be interested if only three people were involved. They did not even know who the men were. In the end Ellis explained that as he had to go to Flotta the next morning, perhaps they could combine Hal's inside knowledge with any observation he could make. Maybe between them an idea may emerge.

Ronald and Ingrid Flett, Hal and Vaila's parents, gave the impression of being well established, confident and kindly folk. Ellis thought they would be exactly the sort of people to whom neighbours would go to for advice and comfort for their troubles. They certainly gave Ellis a warm welcome and he felt at ease at once. Ingrid asked Ellis to sit next to her at dinner. She asked about his work and what he was doing during his visit as she served the meal, and once everyone had their food, she said she wanted to hear all about the find on Anderson's farm, and how Vaila had got stuck in it. His heart sank. As he was not sure what Vaila had told her parents he felt he had to pick his words carefully. He did not want to alarm them, but neither did he want Vaila to think he was putting her down by making light of something she must have found frightening.

"Hasn't Vaila told you all about it?" he asked.

"No, she just said she had got stuck and you had had to pull her out. A bit like caving she said, but as she has never been caving I think there is more to the story. It sounds as if you were the hero, so you must be the one to tell me." Ellis caught a quick wink from Hal who clearly was enjoying Ellis' embarrassment. Ellis did not feel like a hero, quite the opposite. "Well," said Ellis, "seeing you want the whole story I had best tell you."

So he first explained why they were looking down the shaft that James Anderson had found. He described it as like a small round tower, but going down into the ground instead of upwards. He explained that he especially wanted to look inside it, because of its apparent similarity to Minehowe. He described how he had found the tunnel. He explained that his shoulders were too wide to enable him to get in, and when he was about to settle for what photos he could take, he found Vaila had joined him in the first chamber and insisted in exploring the tunnel herself.

"I should have stopped her there, and certainly should not have allowed her to go into the tunnel." He said "I really have to apologise to the family for not realizing that it might be dangerous. I feel guilty about that."

"Nonsense," said Ingrid, "knowing Vaila, you would have had an impossible job to stop her."

Hal laughed "You don't know Vaila, Mum's right I doubt if you could have stopped her. Vaila was always the one to climb cliffs, wade out to get some bit of flotsam, or is it jetsam? She would always accept any dare especially when we were at school. The more I told her not to, the more she was keen to accept the challenge!"

Vaila smiled "As I took no notice whatever of both Hal and Ellis telling me not to go into the tunnel, it was my fault

I got into trouble, and it was you, Ellis, who got me out when I hardly deserved all you did."

Ellis continued by telling them how he had used the jack to free her so he could pull her out. "Can I add this" said Ellis when he had finished the story, "You have a remarkable daughter. She did not scream when the lintel fell on her. She did not panic, she lay still when I asked her, without protest and remained so when I had to push the jack between her and the wall. She never gave any sign that it was hurting her, even though it must have been quite painful, not the smallest groan, cry or anything, until she was out of the tunnel – and then it was in relief at being free. She is the bravest girl I've ever met."

"Perhaps," said Ronald, "but was she remarkably brave or just remarkably silly? You will not do that again I'm thinking, Vaila. Ellis, you clearly did a great job and I hope she thanked you for it – I certainly do."

"Can we change the subject? " Said Vaila, looking embarrassed.

Ellis smiled and turned to Ingrid. "Tell me about the choir and the concerts you are singing in at St Magnus Festival." They then talked about the music for most of the meal.

After coffee Ellis made a move to go. But Vaila asked him what he was doing the next day.

"Just one visit; as I mentioned in the office, I should go to Flotta to look at the World War buildings, and especially what is left of the YMCA as a result of a request to Treasures of Scotland to try to restore them. I gather there is not much to see, and I cannot believe that it is worth any form of restoration, but that is what I have been asked to check. I have a permit to go to Golta already, where the ruins are. There is an early ferry I believe and as I have to be back to collect my stuff from the hotel, in time to catch the late afternoon flight home I'll need to get on with it. I hope I can use the office car to the ferry, but presumably I'll have to walk once on the island."

Hal said "Why don't you come with me? I must catch the early ferry and will also be returning by the midday one. So you will be back in Kirkwall for a late lunch and in time to get to the airport. I have another idea too. I will lend you one of the company bikes, it will save you time."

"Thanks, that's ideal."

Ronald said "Have you seen the weather forecast? It looks as if there will be a haa in the morning; will that spoil your plans Ellis?"

"Only in the sense that it will be hard to find the places I should be looking at"

"I could show you where they are," said Vaila "if Magnus will let me go with you. I will ring him at once." Without waiting for a reply she left the room, to return in a few minutes. She giggled "He says he'll let me come with you, so long as I make sure you catch that plane, as you are disrupting the work of the office. I take that to mean I am to take you to the airport too. He said to tell you that if you abducted me, he'd tell your boss, sack me and choose an ugly secretary next time! He's always teasing me! Anyway, we'll go with Hal, so come here promptly at 8 and we will leave straight away. When we are back in Kirkwall, I'll pick up the office car to take you to the airport, so you should have no problem catching your 15.35 flight."

Having thanked his hosts and wished everyone good night Ellis walked back to the hotel, remarking to himself that it had been some day; the waiter who told him off for talking about the six kippers, as well as having to pull Vaila out of the underground tunnel, the meeting and all he heard behind the display, never mind discovering that there was a plot and a local spy too – and then, if they were right, meeting him, and then the embarrassment of having to tell the family about the rescue at dinner. Surely it had to be a simpler day tomorrow. As he fell asleep he found himself thinking that he would have liked more time in Orkney.

Flotta

Ellis was in the tunnel. It was very dark and he was hemmed in by the walls. He heard three men plotting to catch Vaila. One of them was sleazy Simon, who was saying they should hand Vaila over to him, as he had the social skills to deal with her. Ellis pushed up the ceiling of the tunnel, which seemed to be slowly falling in on him. He had to get out of it as fast as he could. He had to rescue Vaila from the plotters. He really had to fight to get out and all the time Simon was telling him he must improve his technique, but how could he do that if the waiter at the other end of the tunnel would only give him kippers? If he didn't have the kippers, the waiter said, he would never get out in time to save Vaila. It was bad enough to be trapped in the tunnel, but now he seemed to be tied up as well. At last he managed to get untied so he could roll out of the tunnel into the first chamber where he could climb out. Half way up the ladder he realized two men with foreign accents were following him, grabbing his feet. He kicked out to free himself, only to fall off the ladder and he hit the bottom of the chamber with a thump.

He was on the floor of his hotel room which seemed as hard as stone. The bedclothes were in a mess and the heavy curtains across the window obscured nearly all the light, leaving just a thin shaft from between them. The nightmare made him shiver. He got up from the floor, sat on the bed and checked his alarm clock. It said 4 am. He sorted out the bed and got in again. It felt cold and unwelcoming, so to recover he ran his mind over the events of the last two days. He felt as if he had done a great deal, yet thought he had still not achieved much for Treasures of Scotland. He had enough to report on the underground chamber, but doubted if it would be considered of much interest, but until he could see the photos it was hard to be sure. He could record that the paths seen so far were in reasonable order, but that was about all, not much so far. He hoped he could find more interesting things on Flotta. Perhaps the regional office would appreciate an enthusiastic comment concerning the helpfulness of the Orkney Office. He certainly wanted both his boss, and Magnus to think his trip had been worthwhile.

Ellis arrived at the house promptly at 8, on a bright dry morning. Vaila and Hal were waiting for him by Hal's car. As he wished them good morning, Magnus rang on Vailla's mobile and wished them luck and asked what time Vaila would be back in the office after taking Ellis to the airport, and then sent them on their way.

As Hal drove, Vaila asked about the Inverness Office; how many worked there and what they did. Ellis asked about life on Orkney, and whether Vaila would always want to stay there.

"I would like to see the world," Vaila said, "but Orkney would always be home." The conversation took them all the way to Houton for the Flotta ferry, MV Hoy Head. The other ferry was faster but the vehicle ferry suited their business on this occasion. There were only a few passengers, but Hal told Ellis that it would be quite different when the shift changed at the terminal.

To Ellis' surprise the haa that had been forecast was restricted to the eastern part of Scapa Flow, and was drifting away from the western side of Flotta, blown by a gentle south westerly. Vaila pointed out the area where the wartime buildings were, but they were still hidden. The oil terminal filled the view ahead and to the west.

Ellis was astonished at the sheer size of the terminal. Just to their left was the pier where the oil tankers berthed. Beyond it were huge tanks, dozens of them, although he could not tell how far they stretched because the haa kept swirling back and forth. As well as the tanks, there were all sorts of other buildings and structures, including a flare stack.

"About 10% of the UK's oil comes through here," said Vaila. "It comes and goes both by tanker and pipeline. They process some of it here, but I'm afraid you'll have to ask someone else for more detail than that. The great thing is that while it gives a lot of employment locally, and to men from elsewhere, being on Flotta, it has no real impact on any other part of Orkney. Flotta, which means Flat Island was never very attractive anyway."

"It makes a few wartime ruins seem insignificant doesn't it?" Ellis replied "I expect you can tell us more of all the oil processes Hal?"

Hal laughed, "I doubt it, as my maintenance work involves everything except the oil things. Places like the accommodation blocks, the offices, roads and perimeter fence. The site is 500 acres or so, quite enough to keep me busy. They should really make his post full time, but I do not mind because I am always being asked by lots of folk to mend things."

When the ferry docked, Hal took them to a shed where they chose two of the company bikes. "It's a bit far to the YMCA site for you to be back in time for the ferry if you walk. The company keep bikes here for staff which, on this big site, are a good way to get about. I hope you have your pass, Ellis. Here's mine for you, Vaila, with a note to tell anyone who asks that I have authorized your use of it to save you time. You can ride as fast as you like through the haa once you are through the terminal, as no one else is going to be on that road. It goes nowhere. I expect the haa will lift before long anyway."

The weather seemed as if it would cooperate to start with and Ellis was starting to wonder what the fuss had been, until they got to a small rise in the road. Beyond it wisps of a haa were coming to meet them. As they rode it grew thicker until visibility was only around twenty meters. Vaila said that it was enough however, it would not be difficult to find their way.

Quite suddenly two men appeared out of the mist walking towards them.

"Where have they come from?" asked Vaila, but as she did Ellis recognized one of them: Grumpy, the man from his flight. He was dressed for the country in an Irish tweed jacket. The second man had a beard and Ellis thought he could well be the man who had met Grumpy at the airport with a green car. In contrast to Grumpy he had the appearance of a seaman, wearing a dark blue reefer jacket. The two were clearly surprised and a bit annoyed to see them, but they were too close to avoid meeting.

"Good morning." Ellis greeted them.

The grumpy one grunted and stepped to the side as if to let them pass, and then hesitated. "What are you doing here?" and perhaps feeling his question might be turned back on himself, continued "The fog is thicker a short way further on, at the end of the road; it ends rather suddenly. You could

54

easily get lost and find yourselves on the stone jetty, which is slippery. You might fall in."

"We are not going to the end, we have come to inspect the remains of the world war YMCA."

"In this fog? You can't see anything let alone do anything, so I'll wish you luck looking for it. We will carry on."

Ellis could not think how to ask the pair why they were on the road without being nosy, so wished them good-bye and they rode on.

When the men were out of earshot, Vaila said "There is nothing beyond us, except the St Vincent pier. They have either been here some time and are returning or they must have come in a boat, but surely they would just have got lost trying to come ashore in a boat?"

"It might be easier than you think. With a compass and a sat nav it would be possible, and if they came from a big yacht or other boat with radar and radio communications they could have been directed."

"Best of luck, I wouldn't fancy it. I suppose they'll be here for a while. But why would they come at all?"

"Perhaps I am dramatizing something simple, but I can't help wondering if it has something to do with the plot. They can explore in this haa with little chance of being seen. They certainly looked unhappy at our being here, if not quite guilty about something. They certainly were not expecting to see anyone."

Vaila shrugged her shoulders and then pointed to the right; "The remains of the YMCA are just over there. Follow me."

They left the bikes by the road and walked a few yards off the road and then came to a wall about a metre high. They could only see a few metres of it because of the haa. So they followed the wall until they came to five wide steps leading upwards, but there was nothing beyond them. Ellis said "I suppose this must have been the front entrance. Is this really all that is left? This wall must have been no more than the foundations. Of course the building itself was wooden, according to photos I have seen. Is there not supposed to be the large chimney somewhere?"

"Yes, at the back." So they followed the wall round and soon found the chimney. It was impressive in its size, but that seemed about all one could say of it. Ellis looked at it carefully, and noted that it was very substantial, did not seem to have any cracks, nor other signs that might suggest it was liable to fall, but he could not see that there was any point attempting to maintain or restore, either chimney, the wall, or the steps, when there seemed little else of the building left. The main problem was that to give any idea of what it might once have looked like, it would have to be rebuilt – which was not restoration but reproduction. Nor could he think that anyone would want to come all that way and obtain a permit to see it. It was not as if it was one of a collection of places of interest, or that Flotta was an attractive island. He asked Vaila if there was any museum in Orkney that told the story of the military and naval role Flotta played in the wars.

"There is certainly a good one at Lyness on Hoy, and I think there was another on Burray. The Hoxa Head battery is in tourist brochures and there is a good view over Flotta from there too."

Then" he said almost to himself, "I see no real point in doing anything more here. A bit disappointing in a way, as I have little positive to put in my report, but one has to accept reality."

"Talking of reality, Ellis, I think the haa is lifting. I have been wondering why those men warned us off going to the pier. Now maybe we will be able to see from here. I'll climb on the wall, that could help."

She climbed up but turned to Ellis calling "Nothing visible yet, maybe in 20 minutes or so. Ahh...!" The last exclamation was because she had missed her footing and fell back off the wall. Ellis jumped towards her trying to catch her but the only result of his efforts was that she fell against his shoulder and they both ended up on their backs, side by side in the thick grass at the foot of the wall.

"Are you OK?" He was immediately relieved when she laughed. "Once again you have had to rescue me – or at least break my fall."

He sat up, lent on one elbow and looked down at her, he found her irresistible and without thinking of what he was doing, bent down and kissed her.

He felt instantly embarrassed at what he had done. "Oh I'm so sorry. I cannot think what came over me, I shouldn't have done that – it's probably sexual harassment at work or something. That was dreadful of me I really am so sorry." Vaila just laughed, but when she saw he really was confused by his own impulsive kiss, and even a bit red in the face, she sat up and kissed him in return.

"There, now we are equal; you will be had up for harassment and I will be had up for being a temptress.

Anyway it's a nice change. Simon would have tried a lot more than that.

"We had better get back to work, before worse happens. The grass is too wet to lie on anyway!"

They looked right round the rest of the site, and then at the battery site nearby. Nothing Ellis saw changed his mind that there was anything here worth keeping, let alone restoring. As the haa had still not cleared enough that they could see the pier, he suggested they return to the ferry in good time.

As they rode back, however, the haa did slowly melt away and the sun shone. With the increased visibility Ellis looked around Scapa Flow. Apart from Hoy, beyond Flotta to the west, the islands around this great natural harbour are low lying and dotted with white painted houses and farm steadings. There were a few boats, fishing boats Ellis thought, and it was an idyllic peaceful view. He noticed the masts of a boat, presumably a yacht round the headland but could not see its hull.

Ellis was so enjoying the view, riding in companionable silence with Vaila, that he took little notice of the two men walking towards them, until Vaila pointed out that they were the same two that they had met an hour or so before.

The grumpy one spoke to Ellis "Have you been to the end then?"

"No, we came to inspect the remains of the YMCA as we mentioned when we saw you earlier. It once stood over there," Pointing to the site they had just left.

"Why are you so interested in that?" asked the second man. Ellis seeing him more clearly than he had earlier, was sure he was the bearded man he had seen with Grumpy at the airport when he had arrived

"I am from Treasures of Scotland," explained Ellis, whilst puzzled as to why the beard should take such an interest in the ruin. "We had someone studying the history of Scapa Flow in the World wars – it was suggested we restore it. But it is far too far gone for that."

Grumpy replied, "Then you – your organization – will not be coming here again?"

Ellis got the impression that Grumpy really meant that he did not want them to come back.

"No, do you have an interest in it too then?"

"No, no," this time it was the beard that spoke, "Just curious because we sometimes anchor round the headland; it is good holding ground for a large yacht such as *Gaia Marina*, and we can get ashore to stretch our legs, as we are doing now."

"Is that the large green ketch?" asked Ellis. "I saw it from the plane when we came in."

"That's right. But we had better be getting back. We sail for the south first thing tomorrow. Cheerio." And without waiting for a reply they walked on towards the end of the road.

"If I recognize them," Ellis said, "they presumably recognize me. Perhaps Grumpy, who thought me harmless behind the screen, is having second thoughts."

"Does it matter?"

"Not to me, and if they are sailing soon, not to them either I would have thought. We may never see each other again after all. But I am still curious; I still do not know what this kipper thing is all about – or even if it really is a plot at all. We would need to do a lot more detective work to uncover the mystery. Meeting those two does suggest that the yacht has something to do with it."

They met Hal at the pier, returned by the ferry, picked up his car and headed for Kirkwall. Hal dropped them off near the office, so Vaila could pick up the office car, and she stopped at the hotel to pick up Ellis' bag. As it was lunchtime he suggested they had something in the bar. "After all I am on expenses, and I cannot see there could be any objection to my treating you when you have spent so much time driving me around and guiding me to the places I needed to visit." He smiled at her. "It's hardly a candle-lit dinner for two!"

Somehow conversation flagged as they ate, as it can whilst waiting for a journey to start. It wasn't until they were back in the car heading for the airport that Vaila asked when he thought he would come again.

"I don't know, I can't think of any excuse for a return visit all that soon. I wish I could, as all our adventures have been most enjoyable. If I may say so, being with you too has been – I don't quite know how to put it – perhaps sort of special. You are such good company. I won't forget this trip for a very long time, and would it be cheek to add that I won't forget you either?"

Vaila glanced at him, "Oh yes you will, especially when you get home to your girlfriend."

"As I said to Simon yesterday, I haven't got a girlfriend at the moment, and I bet you I will remember."

"I bet you will not – how can you prove to me you will remember me?"

"Have you got your own e mail address? Tell me what it is and I promise to keep in touch that way. Then you will know I am remembering you."

"OK it's *vailaf@gmail.com* I'll write it down for you."

"No need I can remember that. Here we are at the airport. You need not wait for the flight to be called, I am sure Magnus would like you back as soon as possible."

"Maybe, but I should surely stay with my rescuer until he must go; it would be rude not to see you into the airport building at least."

There were quite a few folk around the car park and terminal because an incoming island flight had just arrived, and the Inverness plane was just landing. They got out of the car and Ellis retrieved his bag from the boot.

"Ellis, would you do me a favour?"

"If I can. What would that be?"

"I see behind you – don't look round – two friends of Simon's. I want to send a clear message to him to ensure he understands I am no longer interested in him. Could we kiss good bye – and could we make it look really passionate? After all it was him who called you my new boyfriend and I'd like him to think that you really are."

"It was the only thing he said that I liked. He didn't mean it as a compliment but I took it as one. Maybe if I make a good job of pretending, next time - who knows?"

She did not reply. But they did as she had suggested.

When on the plane he smiled to himself. It was quite easy to give an Oscar-winning performance when you found it such a pleasure, and even better when you are not quite sure if she was a first class actress, or she meant it when she kissed him back.

Later that night, in bed as she waited for sleep, Vaila wondered if Ellis had kissed her the way he had just because she had asked him to. Could he have had such an effect on her if it had only been a charade? She did not feel at all guilty for the lie; surely the lie was justified?

Interlude

Gmail   Back Archive Spam Delete   Move to   labels
More   **1 OF 76**   ◁▷   o

Compose   Hello   Inbox X

Inbox   **ELLIS MACKENZIE**

ellismack@gmail .com   2106 (1 hour ago)

REPLY   Sent mail   to me

Hi Vaila, here I am home and reasonably dry (it's raining) after a boring flight. No kippers, not even any tea, and I am E mailing you to ensure I will win our bet! By the way you never told me what my prize would be, so please think of something nice.

Amongst all my E mails on my home computer, is one from my mother. She thinks I have forgotten her if I do not write her E mails frequently, not least as having just got a tablet she wants to play with it! That's two of you demanding my attention – as Magnus would say, how I suffer!

I'll E again when there is something to say.

Ellis

Vaila Flett   4 hours ago
To me

Thanks for your E mail Ellis. Funny, but I was waiting for your Email to
tell me what I win from our bet. The problem is that if I win it will be
because you've forgotten about me, so how will I get anything?
Hal tells me that he has to see the big boss at the terminal, and is very
puzzled about it. I hope there is no problem for him.
Vaila

Ellis MacKenzie   2 hours ago
To me

Hi Vaila, I am sure Hal has nothing to worry about, in seeing the big
man. May be it's promotion.
I spent much of today looking at the photos we took in the
underground chamber and the tunnel. Putting them on the office
computer I can enlarge them and improve the detail and that way see
so much more.
They are extraordinary. Comparing the shot down the tunnel before
you went into it, and the last one I took just before removing the jack –
after you had climbed out. It looks as if the lintel that fell on you was
held up by a loose stone pillar. One might reasonably think that it was
set like that on purpose, which in turn suggests that whatever the
whole structure was for, the idea of its builder might well have been

that the second chamber should be sealed. Perhaps a place where valuables could be put in times of danger? People in those times, right up to the Viking period, might well have thought of something like that. I do not know anywhere else like it, not even Minehowe. Of course all this is pure speculation, but it does suggest Mr Anderson's find is more significant than I first thought. We will see what the boss makes of it.

Ellis

Vaila Flett   3 hours ago

To me

Dear Ellis, I loved your E mail, certainly all you say about our underground chamber. If it turns out to be famous I hope you will call it 'Vaila's Folly'!

But there is bad news for Hal. Apparently someone has reported him for not doing his job properly and there is to be an investigation. Hal just doesn't understand it. He has not been told who complained, nor what evidence whoever it was produced. The one good thing is that his immediate line manager has the job of looking into it, and Hal thinks he is a very fair minded man. It has come out of the blue, when Hal thought he was doing well. He is to speak to Uncle John, Mum's brother, who is a solicitor as to how he should defend himself.

Vaila

Ellis MacKenzie   2 hours ago
To me

Hello Vaila, I am really sorry to hear of Hal's predicament. I cannot believe he has done anything wrong. If it's any help I would suggest that he should ask for both the details of anything he is supposed to have done wrong, and the name of the person who has complained. If for any reason they will not tell him, then it is an anonymous accusation which should be ignored. But I wonder what the company attitude will be, they may be concerned if the accusation has anything to do with safety. If there ever was an accident and the accuser was able to say that they had ignored a whistle blower – even an anonymous one – it could cause them problems. As he has always been so helpful maintaining things for many folk, I am sure Hal will have a great deal of support on Orkney even if the company do sack him.
Ellis

Vaila Flett   5 hours ago
To me

Thank you so much, Ellis, for your kind words. I decided to tell Hal that I had E mailed you about the problem and he appreciated your kind thoughts too. As it happens Uncle John, said something similar. I found you both very comforting. Please keep writing; I seem to have a regular need of your kindness.

Love Vaila

Vaila Flett   2 hours ago

To me

Dear Ellis. Here I am again. I thought you should know at once that Hal came home with a mixture of relief and thunder tonight. His line manager had a long talk with him about the complaint which was about his supposed lack of maintenance to the perimeter fence around the terminal. Hal was asked to comment and he replied that he would be glad if a full inspection could be made of the fence, along with his own report, sent in only a week ago. His boss agreed to that. Hal then asked if the company actually knew who the complaint came from. His boss said that they did, but as the letter was marked confidential and the man specifically said he did not want his identity revealed, it had been decided to withhold the name from Hal. His manager said "Do you have any enemies, anyone who might want to get you into trouble?" Hal remembered Simon's threat when we all met at the meeting – you'll remember that, Ellis. Hal therefore said "is it Simon Smith?" The reply was "I cannot tell you, so I cannot deny it either," and suggested Hal did not ask more questions.
Ellis, we are both now furious with that worm. Just because he didn't get the job. I wish I'd hit him even harder at that dance.

Thank goodness I refused to go out with him any more – I wish I had never gone out with him at all.
So you have a very cross Vaila writing to you tonight.
Love Vaila.

Ellis MacKenzie   2 hours ago
To me

I bet you look magnificent when you're cross – so long as it is not with me!
Seriously, I am so glad that Hal is off the hook. What a nasty thing for Simon to do. I would not be surprised if he had a second motive; to upset you as well as Hal. He knows fine that you are as close as brother and sister can be, and he will still be mad at you for that dance incident. You made him look a fool. He will also be frustrated at the only (?) girl who has turned him down; he seems to think all girls would melt in his charms.
Ignore me if you like, but I would suggest neither of you do anything to alert SS that you know what he did. He is, after all, a spy for the plotters, and we did think they would be back sometime. We might learn something. It will be good for you both too, to hold the trump card; you know what he has done, and that it did not work, whilst he thinks he has had his revenge without you knowing it was him.
To move to a better subject. Have you told Magnus of my ideas on Vaila's folly?
Your own archaeologist x

Vaila Flett   1 hour ago
To me

Once again, Ellis. You seem to have a knack of writing exactly
what I want – need – to read! I assure you I have no intention
of speaking to SS ever again; he will not be surprised, so will not
suspect. If we ever meet him again you will have to do the
talking.

I told Magnus this morning what you said about Vaila's Folly.
He was very interested and asked if you could E mail copies of
the photos to him.

Being Magnus, he quickly realised that we must have been E
mailing each other on our home computers – so you can
imagine what fun he has had teasing me about my new
boyfriend, as he now calls you! Just as well I have not used the
office network for our correspondence! I am thinking about
what revenge I can take on both Magnus and you for teasing
me. Where can I get a medieval thumb screw?
Love Vaila

Dear Vaila, I'm honoured that Magnus should call me your boyfriend. That's twice someone has done that, all in so short a time. It must be true! Anyway I have sent Magnus the photos via the office E mail, and will be interested in his views on Vaila's Folly.

Now, how about this. I have had the best news a boyfriend could have. I had an E mail from HQ telling me that I have not yet taken any of my holiday entitlement, and I must do so within the next 6 weeks, or lose it. I spoke to the boss about it and arranged to be off for the St Magnus festival in a fortnight's time plus 2 weeks afterwards – 3 weeks in all! Having looked at the web site I have picked out 2 concerts straight away. The opening concert in which both your Mum and Magnus' wife are singing in the Mozart Requiem choir and a Bach concert the following week. Because it is so soon, I cannot book on line, so wonder if you could get me 2 tickets for each? Is there anything else you would recommend? Get 2 tickets for anything you think interesting. There must be someone who would like to come with me..... I'll pay for the tickets when I arrive.

I will come by my faithful if very second hand car on the ferry from Scrabster, 15th June, arriving 2.20.

Looking forward to seeing you.

Your boyfriend X

PS I know where you could get a thumb screw but it isn't in my interests to tell you!

Ellis, I am so excited by your news, it will be marvellous to see
you for three whole weeks, much better than E mailing. You
didn't say where you would stay, so I asked Mum if you could
come here. She said yes at once – she doesn't always - so I
think you are still popular for pulling me out of Vaila's Folly. She
is always keen to talk music, so you got brownie points for that
too. Please accept!
I can get the tickets. Don't you _dare_ take anyone else but me!
There is a reception after the opening concert which would
enable you to meet Uncle John. He is bound to have some
interesting ideas about our 'adventure' no doubt about that.
Apart from Auntie Sally, Dad, Hal and Inga will all be there too
as well as Magnus & Margaret.
In the meantime, I am having lunch with Uncle John just before
your ferry arrives, so I will take the bus to Stromness, and will
be waiting for you in the first layby as you drive off the ferry. I'd
hate to miss you and have to get the bus back. Look out for me.
Hal thinks he saw SS in, of all things, a green car the other day.
Incidentally Gaia Marina is still away, so far as I know. All seems
quiet for the plotters, although I sneaked into the Kirkwall
Hotel the other day and your kippered waiter is still there. I am
not sure he remembers who I am, but he was definitely the
man who came into the office asking about our archaeologist.
Love from your excited girlfriend Vaila XX

Ellis MacKenzie   2 hours ago
To me

My dear Vaila, A quick line to thank your Mum so much for
inviting me to stay and I would love to. How kind she is. Does
she realise that I have become your boyfriend curtesy of
Magnus and even Simon? Whilst I am sure one should not wish
time to pass quickly, I am counting the days. Music, adventures,
no work, never mind a private guide to Orkney – what more
could I want?
See you soon.
Love, your archaeological boyfriend. X

The Concert

Vaila had phoned her Uncle John earlier in the week because she was worried that they might be sitting on important information with regard to all that Ellis had overheard. Uncle John, being a solicitor, would, she was sure, know what should be done. He had invited her to lunch at his home, not least because his wife Sally had said that it was ages since she had seen Vaila.

So Vaila talked to Sally whilst helping her to make the lunch and then, whilst they eat it, Vaila explained her concern, telling Uncle John what they knew, and their decision to keep it to themselves at least until *Gaia Marin*a returned. She explained that she wanted to be sure they had done the right thing.

"Well Vaila, you were certainly right to ask me, but I do not think you have done anything wrong. When it comes down to it you can offer little evidence, and as you do not have any clue as to what your plotters are up to, I cannot see what any of the authorities can do. The Company always keeps a strong security team; they assume the worst as a matter of course so are unlikely to be caught out. As it happens the manager of the terminal, whom I have met a few times, is coming to the opening concert on Saturday. If you are going to the reception afterwards, there may be an opportunity to introduce you to Mr. Triscoll and we can then tell him your story informally."

"Oh yes Uncle, we are all going to support Mum of course, and will be at the reception too."

"Good. I am also curious about Simon Smith's involvement. Can I ask you a rather personal question?"

"Of course, Uncle."

"I believe Simon was your boyfriend. Is he still?"

"Definitely not, Uncle. I made a mistake going out with him, and parted with him when he could not behave himself. For some reason he seems to think I will go back to him as his girlfriend however often I tell him that I do not want to have anything further to do with him. He won't take no for an answer." She said it so hotly that Uncle John smiled as she added. "Now he has been trying to get Hal into trouble at work. He failed but I hope he was not trying to take my refusal out on Hal."

"I am very glad you have told me about that and especially that you will have no more to do with him, not least as I had problems with his father. I had best tell you about it.

Alfred Smith came to Orkney many years ago from the South, I am not sure exactly from where. He got a job with a haulage company, driving Lorries. He had great charm, and was very persuasive. He made good use of these abilities, in the way he persuaded several local folk to give him money. He was one of those people who could sell sand in the desert. I looked into recovering some of it for his victims, but he had been clever; he had done nothing illegal, and even gave some of it back. Such a glib talker he was, that some victims continued to think he was a really helpful and nice man.

Then he took up with a gullible local girl, and she became pregnant, and of course the result was Simon. His driving work took him off Orkney for longer and longer periods. Rumour suggested he had other girls elsewhere, but he had married Simon's mother, and I am not aware that he ever divorced her. His only saving grace was that he appears to have supported them generously, although with whose money I cannot be sure. I still believe he is a disreputable and unacceptable character, and your experience suggests Simon is a chip off the old block. So I am relieved you have dismissed him."

Vaila looked at her watch as she had done already a few times.

"You have plenty of time to walk to the ferry terminal." Said Uncle John, smiling. "Might it be that you are meeting your archeologist off the ferry?"

"You knew?"

"I guessed. Your Mum said you had a friend staying, you have just mentioned him in the account of your sleuthing, but mostly you were spotted by a friend of mine saying good bye to him with some enthusiasm at the airport a few weeks ago."

Vaila blushed, then laughed. "There are no secrets here, are there?" and told him that she had asked Ellis to kiss her good bye just to impress some of Simon's friends, who were watching; it was just an act. She was not sure if he entirely believed her.

"Well, he sounds, from what your Mum has told me, a very nice man and we certainly would not want to keep you from him."

"Thank you so much for an excellent lunch Uncle, it has been very reassuring to talk to you and have your advice. I'll just help Sally with the dishes before I go. We'll look forward to seeing you both at the concert."

"I will look forward to it too. I would very much like to meet this archeologist of yours." Vaila noticed the twinkle in his eye.

She stood by the first point at which a car could stop when coming off the ferry, and carefully checked each car as it passed, as Ellis had not told her what his car looked like.

One rather smart car slowed down, as if the driver was thinking of offering her a lift, but his wife clearly scolded him for having such a thought and it moved on.

Then she saw the man she was looking for.

Ellis stopped beside her leant over and opened the passenger door. "Great to see you – jump in" he said. When she was settled he added "Have you by any chance organized some of Simon's friends to see us? Because if not I'll have to find a reason myself for greeting you as a boyfriend should."

He kissed her then smiled at her. "On second thoughts who needs an excuse?" and chuckled at her embarrassment.

"I'm sorry, but I have a confession to make; none of Simon's friends were at the airport, I just wanted to be sure you would remember me. However friends of Uncle John did see us, he told me when I was having lunch with him, which was a bit embarrassing".

He laughed, "Don't be sorry, I wasn't sure if you would approve of a goodbye kiss, especially after my earlier *faux pas*. You had told me you were off men too. So the favour you requested solved my dilemma. I would have remembered you anyway, but it gave me a nice warm glow all the way home. It also helped ensure I would win the bet. Now, what's this about Uncle John? I didn't meet him last time did I?"

She told him about Uncle John and all that she and her uncle had talked about over lunch, only omitting his comment about Ellis himself. She thought she'd keep that to herself for now.

"Interesting," said Ellis, "it would be good to meet him. And what about the dreaded Simon; is he still after you?"

"Oh yes, I am afraid he is. I was just enjoying a break from shopping the other day, in the 'Coffee Pot' café by the cathedral and he appeared and insisted on sitting with me. Once again he asked me out. He was a bit disconcerted when I told him you were coming back to Orkney for three weeks, so I would not be free to do so. He insisted that I would be far better off with him.

"He went on about how he had now left his job at the Flotta terminal and had a new job. He must have forgotten that he said something about it at the meeting when you were here last time. He said he now worked for something called PPP in Orkney, which he expected would make him rich."

"How did he get such a job?"

"Apparently his father knew the President of this organization, and he was now the President's personal assistant. He spent some time telling me of all the things I would have if I would return to him. Rather harshly I told him I was not for sale like some call girl. He protested he did not mean that. He meant he would be able to give me whatever I wanted if I would marry him. I told him that if that was a proposal the answer was 'no'."

"Curious," replied Ellis "how does he think he can get that rich so soon? I wonder what PPP is? I have never heard of it, yet presumably it has some connection with Orkney, if Simon is working for it here."

When they arrived at the Flett's house in Kirkwall he was given a warm welcome by her parents once again, and shown his room, small and comfortable, just what he needed. As they had a cup of tea Ingrid asked Ellis about his holiday plans.

"As much good music as I can afford, and to get to know Orkney better is what I had in mind. I am hoping a local guide will show me round."

"There are lots of tours and guides you could...." Ingrid started to reply and then saw Ellis looking at Vaila.

"Oh, I think I know who you mean! Vaila has acted as guide to visiting cruise ships so I think you will be happy with her local knowledge."

"Well I can always put in a complaint if my guide is not up to the mark!" Ellis said and Vaila made a face at him.

"How is Magnus to do without you for three weeks by the way?" he asked her.

"As soon as you told me you were coming for three weeks including the festival I asked for the same holidays - I too was due time off. Guess what he said?"

"Oh how I suffer"?

"Yes and as he likes teasing me, 'it's that new archeological boyfriend I suppose - no one loves me anymore!'."

"You see, everyone knows your business here. In all fairness he is very kind because it means a lot more for him to do at a busy time, so I did say if he really needed help, I would come in to the office. I teased him back by telling him that if he needed any archeological advice I knew someone who I was sure would help him."

"He's certainly a great guy, you are lucky to work with him."

Ellis came downstairs, having changed for the concert, and met Vaila in the hall just going into the sitting room. He thought she looked stunning. She was wearing a white dress covered in brightly coloured flower prints. She even wore a neckless. He had not seen her wear any jewelry before. He thought he would be envied by all they met, the men anyway, for being lucky enough to have such a beautiful girl at his side. Before they walked to the concert, Vaila's Dad, Ronald, offered them all a sherry, and in a moment when the conversation lagged he asked Ronald if he had ever heard of an organization called PPP.

"It's funny you should ask that. As I see they are mentioned in the Festival programme. I can't quite make out what they are doing. It is billed as a lecture with music. It says that PPP stands for 'Protect the Planet from Pollution' and that it is an NGO. That is a non profit making outfit, literally a Non-Government Organization. It gives them charitable status I believe."

"So is Treasures of Scotland – we certainly do not make a profit as all our income is spent in looking after our properties and interests. We do not get huge salaries; none of us expect to get rich."

Vaila, listening to Ellis' description, said. "But Simon said he would get rich working for them. Is he really likely to do that well from such an organization?"

"Yes it certainly seems odd. I suppose even an NGO might pay high salaries if it judged it would really help their purposes."

"But Simon said his job was as assistant to the President. It does not sound as if he is very senior. Does he have any special skills, or qualifications?"

"At school he was said to be good with computers, but he hasn't got a degree or any special qualifications, so far as I know."

Ronald looked at his watch and then suggested they should set out for the Cathedral, so the conversation ended.

As he settled into his seat next to Vaila, Ellis looked around. St Magnus Cathedral is a magnificent building. It seems as if, for some indefinable reason, it belonged here; it would not be the same if it was anywhere else. Whilst it is owned by Orcadians, and is still a church, it is also the perfect setting for great music. He remembered wondering whether the builders of the Ring of Brodgar, and of this building had similar reasons for constructing them. Both, he thought, would be proud to know how their creation had survived the centuries because they were appreciated, even loved. The beliefs held by the builders of both must have been strongly held, and whether properly understood or not, had both informed and motivated their work, yet they could not have had the same beliefs. Each generation must have felt they had the truth. "What is truth?" he remembered, was Pilate's question, but even he did not get an answer from Jesus, so, Ellis thought, I do not think I'll ever know either. One must just believe.

The orchestra took their places, the choir filed in behind them and the conductor came onto the podium, and the Mozart Requiem began.

The unusual orchestration, no oboes or flutes, a single trombone and, probably fairly revolutionary for the time, clarinets, gives a feel to the work that is perfect to its message. It is impossible to describe. It has to be heard as the first entry of the clarinets explains it all far beyond the ability of words to do so. He thought it was almost heart wrenchingly beautiful and so absorbing that for him his surroundings melted away; the music alone filled him and he was even temporarily oblivious of the girl beside him.

The interval, after the Requiem, allowed him to re-enter the present, and as they walked to the back of the Cathedral to stretch their limbs from the hard seats several people greeted Vaila. She introduced him as Treasures of Scotland's archeologist but for Ellis, not a lot sunk in; all those names and faces were more than a mind so full of music could remember. But he registered that Vaila was popular amongst her peers, and from the expressions on several faces, realized that as her escort, he was being carefully scrutinized. He didn't mind, island life he supposed.

The second half was excellent too but for Ellis, it did not quite reach the same magnificence of the Mozart, so he was able to spot both Ingrid and Margaret, Magnus 'wife, in the choir.

When the concert was over Vaila whispered to Ellis to follow her, and they made their way to a hall next door for the reception. As they entered and took a glass of wine from the tray offered, he saw Ingrid and Ronald, Margaret with Magnus, and Hal beside an attractive girl. He led Vaila in

81

their direction where he congratulated the ladies on their performance. "It is such a wonderful piece, and so well sung that I became totally lost in it. I nearly forgot about Vaila!"

Ensuring Magnus could hear her, Vaila replied, "Oh how I suffer!"

She continued, introducing Inga, "Ellis, this is my best friend Inga, who has had the misfortune to fall for big brother Hal!"

Hal did not miss his opportunity, "Inga, this is Ellis MacKenzie who is taking a considerable risk in coming all the way from Inverness to see piddie sister!"

Inga joined in, replying to Hal "Well at least he's better than the last one. Don't mind us, Ellis, we always poke fun at each other."

He laughed, and said "Ah yes I've heard that you had an irresistible offer from sleazy Simon – how did you manage to say no?" They all had a laugh at that.

Uncle John joined them, again congratulating Ingrid and Margaret. He turned to Ellis, standing beside Vaila and said "You must be Ellis MacKenzie, the archeologist?"

"That's right, and you must be Vaila's Uncle John."

"Indeed, Vaila has told me about your adventures a month or so ago. It certainly sounds as if you had an exciting trip on that occasion. Is this visit for work or holiday?"

"Holiday. I have been keen to come to the St Magnus Festival for some time, and there are also many archeological sites my work has not given me time to explore so I am expecting a well filled time."

"Other attractions too, no doubt!" His twinkle returning. "Now I am longing to hear about all you heard and saw on your last visit. Vaila has told me about it, of course, but it would be good to hear it from you too. I see Tom Triscoll, the Flotta manager over there so would you mind if he also heard your story?"

"I'd be happy to meet him. I might have to look at the war time sites again as they were in a thick haa last time. It would be as well that he knows who I am."

Tom Triscoll was American and clearly proud of it. He greeted John with warmth and enthusiasm, saying how much he was enjoying his time in Orkney.

"So, John, what is the latest thing for you?"

"Can I introduce my niece Vaila, and her friend Ellis Mackenzie? He is an archeologist with Treasures of Scotland. Vaila works for the same organization. They have stumbled on some interesting information which I felt you should hear."

"Great to meet you young folks. Ellis, do you work from the office here?"

"And good for me to meet you too. I work from the Inverness office. Normally I only come to Orkney once or twice a year, as I also cover Shetland, Caithness and Sutherland. But just now I am on holiday, enjoying the St Magnus festival, not for my work.

"So tell me about what John was talking about just now."

"A month or so ago I came on business, amongst other things, to inspect the wartime remains on the Golta peninsular. The afternoon before my permit allowed me to

83

visit that part of Flotta, I went to the meeting your company held about the expansion plans. I was looking at the large map on display when I overheard a conversation behind it. It seemed to fit with a strange phrase I first heard at Inverness airport."

Ellis then went through the story of his last visit from hearing the phrase about the six kippers, to what he had overheard and seen at the meeting. Vaila added a few details. Neither of them mentioned Simon, partly not wanting to bring up his accusation against Hal again.

Uncle John thanked them and asked Tom Triscoll what he made of the story.

"If the plotters, as you call them, really intend something that neither threatens to hurt anyone nor spills any oil, it must be something harmless like a demonstration. As virtually all the employees at the terminal appreciate the jobs it gives them, I do not think we have much to fear, but I will tell our security team, just in case. I do appreciate you telling me about it, because these days you never know what slime balls are out there.

"If you want to have another look at the stuff at Golta or otherwise discover anything else let me know."

He then gave Ellis his card including a number of his private direct phone.

"Thank you. Unfortunately there was such a fog I did not see the sites themselves properly, so I might well need to ask for a permit to look again shortly."

"No problem." Said Triscoll. "What does Treasures of Scotland want to do with the remains?"

"My recommendation was that we should not attempt to do anything with them. Their story can be told at the Lyness museum, but there is so little left of the structures, and so difficult to get to them for visitors, that I cannot see it would be either possible or worthwhile to do anything more than that."

"That's OK. I don't really mind what you do, but I guess it is one less thing to think about for us too. I do hope we will see you around again."

Triscoll left them to speak to other folk in the room.

Uncle John said "I think you have made a good friend there. He is the sort of man who would welcome your call even if it is about a fairly trivial matter, so do not hesitate to use it.

To change the subject, would you be interested in using my boat? Have you sailed?"

Ellis' eyes lit up. "That would be wonderful. I have done some sailing and love it. Perhaps Hal and Inga would like to come too at the weekend. Thank you so much."

"Well," said Uncle John, "I do not get out in her as much as I would like. I am afraid I mainly use the engine and go fishing, but she is fully equipped with sails too. She is a 27 foot ketch called *Solvaig*. She is moored in Hamnavoe. The boatyard in Stromness will sort out all you need, keys and so on. I will tell them to expect you."

After thanking Uncle John again and making detailed arrangements to go for a sail, Ellis, Vaila Hal and Inga moved away, to meet several of their friends gathered on the far side of the room. They welcomed Ellis into their group and they spent some time discussing the contemporary scene in

Orkney and comparing it with all that Inverness offered. Ellis found them all excellent company, and he noted again that Hal and Vaila were clearly popular amongst this circle too.

Meanwhile, when Sally joined him, John spoke to Ingrid and Ronald "I expect you are relieved that Vaila has a better boyfriend than Smith." He said "I know I am."

"Yes. I am afraid we did not like Simon Smith, though we could not quite put our fingers on what it was that put us off. He appeared charming enough. Perhaps a bit too charming? I do not like to quiz her about her boyfriends, she wouldn't like it, but I get the impression that she has fallen out with Simon, and I am not sorry.

"I told you I thought Ellis was a nice man, John. I am much happier that she sees him. As you know she is apt to be a bit too adventurous, as if she was still the tomboy she was at ten years old. Simon seemed quite the wrong sort of man for such an adventurous girl."

"Yes. Does Hal tell you anything?"

"Not really. The pair of them are loyal to each other and don't give much away to their parents! But if Hal did not like Ellis, I am sure he'd tell her, even if he didn't tell us. Vaila asked me if he could stay with us for his holiday and if she is interested enough to want him to stay, I thought we should get to know him better too".

Ronald said "We were impressed with the way he helped her when she had that adventure underground. They must have been e mailing each other ever since that incident. It seems to me that Vaila has met her match so far as adventurousness is concerned!"

Solvaig

The weather was ideal on the day that Vaila, Hal, Inga, and Ellis drove together to Stromness, and parked in the Hamnavoe boat yard. There was blue sky, with just a few white clouds and the wind from the southwest was about force 3, so far as Ellis could judge.

Whilst Vaila and Inga went to organize a picnic, Hal and Ellis were ferried out to *Solvaig* on her mooring by one of the boatmen, Alex. He first showed Hal the engine, telling Hal that the inboard petrol engine was a little temperamental. "It should be fine but there is a problem which I have not yet entirely solved. It should at least get you in and out of harbour, but sometimes, the engine cuts out, and it can be hard to restart until it has cooled off. At other times it just does not start whatever you do . But with patience it ought to be fine. It must be something to do with the carburettor, as it's a good motor most of the time."

"That's fine, I'm reasonably sure I can cope with an unhappy engine. Ellis is keen to get some sailing in, so I suppose that if we have to wait for the engine to cool we can sail, so long as he really knows what he is doing!" He winked at Ellis who replied "I will look forward to sailing without the smell and noise of the engine, but first I'll have a look below."

Ellis checked the equipment and was impressed. There were all the necessary lifejackets, flares and so on, and the standing rigging, sheets and halyards all looked as if they had been recently renewed. The anchor was ready for use if need be, and the cockpit locker had warps, fenders and a few general spares. In the little cabin he found several charts for

Orkney waters, including a detailed one for Scapa Flow. There was even an up to date pilot book. Pretty good for a boat used mainly for a little fishing, if that really was all Uncle John did.

They then dropped the mooring and, on engine, brought her alongside the quay to get all the gear on board, including a full set of sails. As Alex and Ellis were bending on the sails, Vaila and Inga returned with what looked more like a feast than a picnic. All was set.

"The day is reasonably warm, and with a steady south westerly. You should have a pleasant day. Where are you thinking of going?" Alex asked.

I should think we might reach across Scapa Flow and could perhaps have a look at some of the smaller islands. Any special hazards I should watch out for?"

Before climbing the ladder back onto the quayside, Alex said, "There no special problems. The chart will keep you right. Keep a look out for traffic to the Flotta terminal – but the tankers are so big you'll not fail to see one of those if it comes! Have a good time, but," looking at the bags the girls had produced, "don't eat too much!"

Hal started the engine, whilst Ellis took the helm and they eased out of Hamnavoe, an inlet that acts as a harbour for Stromness. It is reasonably wide and simple to navigate except when the Scrabster ferry is entering or leaving. They were not far from the mooring when they saw her coming. Ellis switched on the depth sounder to ensure there was enough depth of water as he steered Solvaig as far to port as he could, just outside the buoyed channel. They passed the ferry without incident. Ellis found *Solvaig* responsive under engine, and in a short time was able to turn eastward between Inner and Outer Holm.

Solvaig was a gaff rigged ketch. About 27 feet long with the graceful lines of a traditional boat from the Northern Isles, double ended and clinker built. Orkney boats, although of the same basic design, tend to be slightly beamier than Shetland models. *Solvaig* was also half decked with a small cabin set mid ships. Largely painted white, she had the top two strakes in red, with her underwater paint matching. A very smart craft indeed to Ellis' delight. Her ancestry, as with all the traditional craft in the northern isles, was undeniably Norwegian – even Viking, and presumably, Ellis thought, that was why she had a Norwegian name.

Once clear of other boats and shipping, Ellis suggested they hoist the sails.

"Don't you like the steady sound of a good engine?" said Hal.

"No," said Ellis smiling "nasty smelly things, engines. Sails are the thing, quiet and you never run out of free fuel."

"You've no idea…" said Hal and was about to launch into an argument when he saw the grin on Ellis' face. "You are winding me up."

"Of course and you nearly fell for it!"

"Are you going to get the sails up, or just talk about it?" Vaila said to Ellis. "You are acquiring Magnus' habit of teasing."

"Oh how I suffer!" said Hal and they all laughed.

Ellis then showed them how the sails were raised. He asked Inga to take the helm, "Inga, we need the boat to point into the wind as we raise the sails, so they do not catch the wind until we are ready. It is best if point a little to one side of the eye of the wind, because it means the boom, this spar here, is less likely to swing across the boat while we are making sail. You will know all about it if your head gets in its way! If you aim for that hill on Hoy there" – and he pointed – "that should about do it."

Once he was confident that Inga understood and could hold the course described, he went forward to the mainmast to prepare the main sail, and hank on the jib. He asked Vaila to raise the jib, showing her the halyard, the rope that did so. He took the main and peak halyards, and matched the rising jib, so the two sails went up together. He then pulled the halyards as hard as he could manage, because, he told the others, that gave the best set to the sails. The sails flapped noisily but harmlessly. He then went to the mizzen mast to raise its sail and when he was satisfied all three sails were properly set, returned to the cockpit.

"Vaila, take the rope that controls the jib, it's called a sheet, that one there on the lee side, and Inga the sheet that controls the mizzen; I will take over the helm and the main sheet. Haul in the jib Vaila. A bit more, yes, that's enough, and Inga try to bring yours in until it is roughly at the same angle to the boat as is the jib. When you have the setting the same on both, you can fasten them to the cleats – those things there – in a figure of eight pattern."

"Now, Hal, you can stop the engine. Hal reluctantly turned the key to stop it. He said he felt they were abandoning their proper means of control over where they went and how fast.

Ellis smiled from beside the tiller, and to the others consternation, stood up and let go the tiller. "Don't worry. We are hardly moving so the rudder isn't doing much anyway." He used both hands to pull in the mainsheet. He cleated it down. As the boat started to move forward he said "Here we go." He turned *Solvaig* off the wind until all three sails caught and were drawing.

Solvaig healed to the pressure of the wind and smoothly accelerated in what felt like appreciation. Just as a horse might enjoy being given his head, *Solvaig* seemed to delight in doing what she had been designed to do. Ellis was amused at Vaila humming to herself the 'Farewell to Stromness'.

"Hal," Ellis said "Is that the Calf of Golta in the distance over there?"

"Yes, from here it looks like an extension of the finger of land going east from the Oil Terminal. Your YMCA ruin might be visible when we are nearer. You do know, don't you, that only a small rowing boat can go between Golta and the Calf. They dumped a lot of the wartime nets and things there when peace came."

"Yes, it's in the pilot book. Where did you see *Gaia Marina*?"

"From the Flotta fast ferry yesterday, it seemed to be circling around Golta as if looking for a place to anchor. Perhaps she went just round the corner?"

"We will go and have a look."

Ellis thought it would take them up to an hour and a half to reach Golta, from Hamnavoe, and suggested they enjoyed lunch as they went. The girls unpacked what they had brought and they eat and enjoyed the sail. With a steady wind it was a very pleasant picnic.

Lunch over and cleared away Vaila and Hal, sitting beside the cabin hatch, were in a deep discussion which Ellis could not hear, so he said to Inga "Would you like to have a go at sailing *Solvaig*?"

"I have no idea what to do."

"That's OK I'll show you.

We are on a reach – that is with the wind coming from the beam, which is the easiest point to handle her. You won't find it difficult. It's not much different to steering than when we are on engine. Once you have the hang of it the others might pay more attention to what we are doing and have a go too. It is only sense that you can all manage it. You never know, I might fall overboard!"

"Please don't. Vaila would never forgive me if I let you do that!"

It didn't take long for Inga to learn and she was soon enjoying being in charge.

"So you are a nurse at the Kirkwall hospital. Do you enjoy that?" Ellis asked, and for a while they discussed life on Orkney in general and the health provision in particular as they sailed.

He saw that she was a little taller than Vaila, and had lighter coloured hair but her voice, with its gentle Orcadian accent, was similar. A most attractive couple of girls and excellent company, Ellis thought.

At that moment, Ellis saw a tanker coming slowly round Roan head, at the end of the Golta peninsular, being guided by two tugs one at the bow and one at her stern. He went below, checked the chart and pilot book, returned to the cockpit with the binoculars he had seen there and Looked at the tanker and then for a buoy, somewhat north of their current course. He soon spotted it and pointed it out to Inga.

"Inga, we will need to leave that buoy to our starboard. Starboard is the right hand side of the boat facing forward. The chart and the pilot book explain that incoming tankers are turned by their tugs around here. By going to the buoy we should be out of their way, and can resume our course when they have passed us."

"What do I do to change course – do the sails need adjusting?"
"It is not a big course change, so just turn to port, and once settled on the right bearing we will ease the sails out, as the wind will then be nearly behind us."

Inga pushed the tiller tentatively away from her, but Ellis said, "No, not that way and he put his hand on hers to show her.

A voice – Hals – called "Ellis; What are you doing, chatting up my girlfriend, and holding hands with her?"

Vaila added "and, Inga, put my boyfriend down!"

"Why have we changed course anyway?" asked Hal – he had not heard Ellis' explanation.

Ellis enjoyed the banter, and felt so at home with them, that he wondered if everyone here was so warm hearted to a mere visitor, what would life be like if he lived in Orkney permanently?

Vaila moved to be beside Ellis and asked him to explain how the boat was sailed, which he did. "Why don't you have a go when Inga gets tired of it?

Inga said "Go on, it's easy and gives you quite a feeling of power. I had better stop anyway or Hal will think I am being disloyal to the real love of his life - engines!"

Vaila took over and they continued on course for the buoy, whilst watching the tanker and its tugs pass. Once they had a clear view past the tanker they saw Gaia Marina at anchor in the bay created by Golta and the Calf, a small isle to the north of Roan Head. Ellis when said "We can now set a course for *Gaia Marina*. We will need to be hard on the wind to do that, so get ready. When we are on the right course *Solvaig* will heel quite sharply, so you should all be on the starboard side to balance her as far as we can. Don't worry about it, she cannot capsize." Vaila, moved to the cabin hatch so she could hold the grab rail there and he took over again. He explained what was needed and then turned to starboard, Hal, Inga and Vaila handling the sheets, to sail as close to the wind as Solvaig could manage comfortably with the wind now well forward of the beam and the sheets hardened. *Solvaig* heeled in reaction to the wind, and she seemed to be sailing much faster. She proved excellent on the wind, the water rushing along the lee side and occasionally taking aboard a wave top. When there was an extra puff of wind waves would splash over the bow, as a shower of white fairy lights flickering in the sunlight.

Ellis chose the eastern tip of the Calf as his leading mark, which meant they were sailing more or less as close to the wind as they could. They were still some distance from *Gaia Marina*, when Ellis saw a speed boat emerge from the far side of the anchored yacht. At the same time, Hal, looking beyond the Calf to the west saw one of the tugs, having finished turning the tanker, heading their way. He pointed it out to Ellis, who watched both the speed boat and the tug carefully, before saying

"I think the tug will pass astern of us quite closely, and ahead of the speed boat if it sticks to a sensible course and speed. I wonder why they are coming towards us anyway."

"Which will get here first?" asked Vaila. "Should we be getting out of the way as we did for the tanker?"

"No need. They can both see us clearly, and will, as far as I can tell, pass us if we all stay on the same course as we are now. We will just keep watching in case I am wrong. The only thing is that I do not think the speed boat can see the tug yet, not until they are clear of the Calf."

"Where is the tug going – why does it not stay with the tanker?" Inga asked.

Hal replied, "Probably St Margaret's, perhaps it has another job there."

"Coming on that course she is certainly intending to go round Roan Head," added Ellis.

They watched the two approaching craft, and it was soon clear that, fast as the speed boat was going, the tug would pass them first. As it came closer they could see that it was a large sea going vessel, the sort that supported North Sea operations and it was obviously very powerful. It was going at some speed, making a considerable wash. It shortly swept past *Solvaig* a little less than a hundred meters away from their stern and then turned round them towards the headland.

"Hold on tight everyone" said Ellis, "we will bob up and down quite dramatically as the wash reaches us."

The first wave arrived and lifted the stern nearly a meter. At this point the speed boat was rapidly approaching *Solvaig* from their port beam, and by now was only 50 meters away as the tug passed them. They saw that there were two men in it, one driving the boat and the other standing beside him, holding the windscreen with one hand and with binoculars in the other, trained on *Solvaig*. They must have seen the tug, it was much bigger than *Solvaig*, but they did not appear to realize the wash it was creating or the danger it could be to their small boat. As the first wave reached them the light speed boat's bow was suddenly lifted up, and combined with its outboard engine driving it fast, it was left partly in the air, twisting on the top of the wave with only the outboard still in the water. The standing man lost his hold on the windscreen and fell across the steersman, both their weight causing it to heel violently and the steersman to loose what little control he still had. The speed boat crashed down in the trough of the first wave, shipping water as it turned sharply to port just as the second wave hit it heavily on the beam. It stood no chance; it capsized and sank in a few brief seconds, leaving its two crew in the water. It all happened so quickly that they found it hard to believe that they had seen anything at all.

The tug was well ahead of *Solvaig* by now and already on course to go round Roan head and Ellis doubted if their crew had ever seen the speed boat.

"Vaila", he called" Can you see the men in the water?"

"One of them yes"

"You are nearest the bow, keep your eyes on him, and point. Do not do anything else. Never take your eyes off him for a second or we will never find him."

"Hal; start the engine."

"Inga, come to the cockpit. Let go the main sheet, just let it flap. It will be noisy but *Solvaig* will slow down."

As they sailed towards the man in the water, now only 25 meters away, Ellis wondered what the problem with the engine was. Hal was having no success starting it. Hal looked up; "Sorry Ellis it won't start. I think I know what it needs, but it will take a little time."

"OK, then just leave it for now. I think we can get to that man on this tack, but we will both have to help him aboard. Vaila, what about the second man?"

"I think I can see him, just beyond the first one, but he is still, and held by his life jacket on his back."

They were soon close to the first man, and Ellis was able to steer just to leeward of him. "Grab him when we are alongside," he said to Hal. "Inga, uncleat the jib sheet and hold it ready to let go as soon as Hal has hold of the man. I will do the same with the mizzen. It may take the three of us to get him on board. Vaila, still keep your eyes firmly on the second man. Ignore what we are doing."

Solvaig behaved like a perfect lady, gently coming alongside the first man in the water. Hal grabbed him but could only hang on, the man's clothes were so full of water that he was extremely heavy. By using about two meters of the tail of the mainsheet, with a bowline under his armpits, and the sheet winch to help to lift him, Hal and Ellis eased him over the combing. They could then roll him into the cockpit. He was just regaining consciousness and thanked them before blacking out again.

"A chance to use your nursing skills, Inga, while we try to reach the second man. Vaila, can you still see the second man?"

"Yes, but he's not showing much sign of life."

"OK – Hal can you pull in the jib sheet there, and I'll do the same with the mizzen. We just want to move forward slowly to get alongside number two. I'll try to have him on the other side, or we will have to move number one. There is no time for that."

As with the first man, the main problem proved to be getting number two on board. He was much harder to lift than the first, because he was both unconscious and a rather larger man. Eventually they managed it in the same way as his companion.

Inga, having looked at both men, and covered them with their spare coats, and some life jackets she found in a locker, said, "We need to get these two at least into a warm bunk, as they have been in cold water – luckily not for too long. This one has hit his head quite hard on something, which is why he's unconscious. Where is best, as it took nearly two hours to get to here from Stromness?"

"They came off *Gaia Marina*, and it is a big yacht, so I think we had best deliver them there. Presumably they have seen us, but I am surprised they haven't sent another boat."

The first man to have been picked up came to, and groggily said to Inga "Sorry, I must have passed out. You are all so kind. I should explain we have never used that speed boat before. I didn't think it so flimsy. I am Euan and my friend is Mark. Is he OK? "

Inga said "I'm glad to see you recovering. Your friend Mark has hit his head but he will be fine if we can get the two of you to somewhere warm fairly quickly."

Ellis told Euan "We'll get you onto your yacht in a few minutes. Just relax for the moment."

He then told Hal and Vaila to reset the sails. "To reach Gaia Marina, we will need at least one tack, as she is now up wind. I'll explain what the plan is as we go along."

Ellis immediately had all the sails sheeted in hard and sailed as close to the wind as possible taking a long starboard tack. Once he felt confident they could get alongside the larger yacht, he put Solvaig about. He asked Hal to put fenders out on the starboard side.

Ellis then explained the problem of coming alongside under sail. They must ensure Solvaig would be only moving very slowly, and because Gaia Marina was swinging to and fro on her anchor, they would have to time their approach to match the swing. Ellis asked Vaila and Inga to be ready to release the jib and main sheets, and Hal to find a long enough rope from the locker, and to take it onto the foredeck ready to throw a line across. He decided the mizzen could be left as it was.

By the time he had finished telling them how he thought they could manage it, they were quite close, and Ellis was glad to see *Gaia Marina* on the end of the swing away from *Solvaig*. This meant that she would now swing towards them and all he had to do was to sail in gently to meet *Gaia Marina*. He asked Inga to release the mainsheet to spill wind from the mainsail. He turned *Solvaig* straight into the wind when he judged she would meet the swinging yacht and told the girls to loosen the jib and mizzen sheets, but to keep the tail of them in their hands in case he had misjudged the turn.

To Ellis' relief, his turn worked exactly as he intended, and *Solvaig* came gently alongside *Gaia Marina* amidships. Hal was able to climb over *Gaia Marinas* rails with the bow line and secure it to a convenient cleat. There seemed no crew on board – certainly none on deck. Once the yachts came together, Ellis too was able to thread *Solvaig*'s stern line through the larger boats rail and onto a cleat, so that the two yachts were rafted together. They took down the main and jib, but left the mizzen to help steady *Solvaig* while they got the two men aboard the bigger yacht.

Ellis was about to climb onto *Gaia Marina* to look for someone on board to help transfer the speed boat crew onto her, when an upper class voice above him said "How very kind of you to rescue our boat crew. They were careless to have capsized, as far as I could see through binoculars. They were very lucky too. Our other two boats with some of the crew are away with the Captain taking the props and so on for our show tomorrow and fetching supplies. Come on board and have a drink before you go." He then turned to a man, who had followed him from below and said "Andy, please arrange to get those two on board. Perhaps get them a hot drink and they can then turn into their bunks, until the others return"

Gaia Marina

Andy looked puzzled and helpless as their potential host walked away towards the stern of *Gaia Marina*.

"There is no one to help, you will have to get them up here yourselves." He said it quietly as if he did not want to be overheard. "I will get them coffee and see their bunks are OK with some extra covers. Sorry." He went to the fore hatch and below. He looked miserable, as if his cares were unending.

Ellis thought Andy would not have been much help anyway and it was just as well that both Euan and Mark were now fully conscious and able to climb aboard *Gaia Marina* with only a little help, although when they did so, he thought they were still a bit shaky from their experience. They certainly shivered from the cold water still dripping from their clothes. But before going below after Andy, they turned and thanked their rescuers profusely.

"Thank you so much for picking us up" Euan said "without you we would have drowned. Mark and I really cannot thank you enough. We hope you do not need it, but if ever you had such an emergency I hope we would be able to help you in return."

Mark added apologetically "I'm afraid we are not used to speed boats. Count me in too for anything we can do for you, anything at all. We owe you our lives." They shook the hands of each of *Solvaig*'s crew in turn and then went below, again via the fore hatch.

From the stern of the large yacht the invitation was repeated as if they were causing a delay. Ellis not only felt they could not refuse the invitation to go on board, but that it might prove interesting anyway. A glance at the others and a nod between them confirmed agreement, so he called back "Thank you, we'd love to, but we must not be long because we need to sail back to Stromness while the wind holds."

He suggested the others went first as he wished to add a short spring[1] between the yachts to keep them apart. Once he had put the spring in place, he bent down to coil the excess rope. He found himself looking through a porthole and was startled to see Simon and Grumpy, playing cards. He quickly moved away to avoid being seen himself.

It certainly removed any doubt that the plot involved Simon and *Gaia Marina*, as well as those they had christened the plotters. They must all be in it together. He wondered why they had stayed below, they must have heard them come alongside, and if they had looked must have seen something from their porthole. Perhaps they had just thought it was the yacht's boats returning. But more immediately he wondered what Vaila's reaction would be should she see or worse meet Simon, or Simon meet her.

He badly wanted to tell her, but he could not resist the temptation to take a moment, as he climbed over the rail on to *Gaia Marina*'s deck, to look around. He was surprised by how large she was; he estimated that she was around 30 meters long. Rigged as a ketch, he could see that she had every refinement that ease of sailing, and crew convenience

---

[1] A spring is a rope from the aft end of the smaller boat to forward of the larger. The current or wind pushes the bow of the smaller boat away from the larger, so they do not rub together.

required. She could probably be sailed by only two or three crew, he thought. Doubtless she was also well appointed below, at least in the main areas. He had not been able to tell in a short glance through the porthole.

He went quickly to the cockpit at the stern, where he saw the others seated. Their host introduced himself as soon as Ellis arrived.

"I am Sir Frank Malloss; and I'm very glad to meet you, not least to thank you for rescuing my men. It was a neat bit of sailing, if I may say so, but why did you pick up my men and even come alongside under sail? Would it not have been easier to use the engine?""

The name Malloss seemed vaguely familiar to Ellis, but he could not place it. At the same time he was anxious to be polite, not least as he hoped to learn more by doing so, and was equally keen to tell Vaila that Simon was on board, so gave little thought to the question. To give him a moment to think, he replied briefly that Solvaig's engine was unreliable, and because the wind was favourable for the purpose, it had seemed the simplest way to do it.

"Would you like one of my people to look at the engine when they return on board?" Malloss asked. Hal quickly but politely refused. He said that it was just a small block in the carboretta which he would clear as they sailed home. It all sounded reasonable, but Ellis felt that Hal just did not want anyone else interfering and wondered why. Perhaps he just did not want to hang around waiting for the crew to get back.

Malloss asked them what they would like to drink and then went to arrange it. In the moment when they were alone, Ellis leant over to Hal sitting next to him and whispered that he had seen Simon and Grumpy and to warn Vaila. Hal just had time to do so. Ellis saw her frown, but she otherwise gave nothing away.

When Malloss returned, and gave them the drinks he said "Please do introduce yourselves, I must know who so nobly carried out the rescue." Each of them gave their names.

When it was Vaila's turn to give her name, Malloss said to her,

"Oh, I have heard of you, a friend of yours is one of our team, and is on board, Simon Smith. I'll give him a call." And he got up and went into the adjacent saloon to do so before Vaila could say anything to him, but she said to the others.

"Why is it that I seem never to be free of that wretched man? If I get the chance I'll make it quite plain to Malloss that he is no friend of mine."

"Unfortunately it looks as if we will have to see Simon, but we are with you, so keep cool. We won't be here long." Hal told her.

"I saw him through a porthole with Grumpy, as I climbed aboard," explained Ellis. "I did not want to say anything in front of Malloss."

Ellis had no sooner said this when Simon came out of the saloon. Smiling broadly, dressed as well as ever, even sporting a yachting cap that would have made the Royal Yacht Squadron proud.

"Hello, Vaila, beautiful as ever I see. So nice of you to drop in to see me, though you really did not need to bring big brother to protect you, a nurse to nurse you, nor especially your pet archeologist."

"Ha ha, be careful of pets, Simon, they sometimes bite." Vaila replied, clearly with no intention to be funny.

Malloss who was just behind Simon, did not appear to have noticed how sharply she spoke. He asked Ellis if he was the archeologist that Simon had told him about, and whether he was working on a site in Orkney.

"I am certainly an archeologist, but just now I am on holiday, enjoying the music festival. And some sailing of course."

"Then you must come and hear our version of Peter and the Wolf. It is part of the fringe programme so you will have the details. Not only am I sure you will enjoy it, it will tell all about our charity PPP and our work. We are dedicated to clearing up all pollution in the world. – Simon is naturally part of my team and involved in the show too of course."

"Thank you for telling us about it; we will certainly come if we can." Ellis quickly replied.

Simon said, "I deal with the lights, projection, amplification and general logistics. I'll be in a sort of enclosure or projection room behind screens at the back of the hall; Vaila, you might like to join me there? I'll be able to explain how everything works – it is really very interesting"

"I had better not," she replied, and wanting to be as cool as Hal had suggested, turned to Malloss and said as if she was revealing a secret between them, "One of Simon's little jokes. He likes to meet me in the dark, but if I fell for that, he would be unable to do his job. He is my EX-boyfriend, and he finds me a painful ice maiden. It would be safer all round if we stay ex and far apart."

Malloss smiled; "You clearly enjoy a little verbal dueling. Anyway I have work to do, so will leave Simon to entertain you. When you want to go, just ask Simon or the crew to let go your lines. See you at Peter and the Wolf. Cheerio. "

Malloss went into the saloon.

Simon could not leave Ellis alone. "I thought you were just a work colleague of Vaila's?"

"So I am, but we are both on holiday just now."

"Don't tell me you ignored my advice not to waste your time with the Ice Maiden?"

"I thought you knew I was coming for the festival; Vaila told you, didn't she?"

Hal joined in with a broad grin; "Ah Simon, did you know that Ellis is now sleeping in our house?"

Simon was taken aback. His face gave away his jealousy.

"On his own I trust?"

"You have a one track mind, don't be silly. That is not a nice thing to say."

"You tease me, so why can I not tease you? But I must be clear Ellis, I don't give up, and I am confident she will return to me when you have gone home."

"That is up to Vaila."

Out of sight of Simon Hal winked at Vaila and then said to him "But Simon, that's impossible as you have not got the essential qualification to win Vaila's heart."

"What do you mean?"

106

"You haven't noticed? " Said Hal, stringing Simon along. "She is only interested in men with a degree in archeology these days."

Simon took him seriously "It's all your fault, Ellis, she never had such thoughts before you came along."

With an undisguised tongue in cheek, Ellis said "Simon, I can recommend a suitable four year course at York University. Surely you wouldn't begrudge the girl of your dreams such a symbol of your wish to please her?"

"Enough," said Vaila "It's all very flattering that you should argue over me, but it's gone on long enough. Please can we set sail for home Ellis, and if you want to be useful Simon, you can cast us off when we are back in *Solvaig*.

Vaila stood up and said "Oh yes, and before you ask, Simon, even when Ellis has gone home, I still won't go out with you, as I told you when you came into the Coffee Pot café, not even if you get an archeological degree." She resolutely walked along the deck and climbed down to Solvaig. The others followed.

Ellis was not sure if Simon thought it would make things difficult or he was just in a hurry to be rid of them, but even before Ellis could raise the mainsail, Simon had cast off all the lines and Solvaig drifted away from Gaia Marina.

"How kind he is," said Ellis cynically and quietly, and then loudly called "Good bye Simon, have a nice day."

They soon had all the sails set and *Solvaig* picked up the wind. Ellis took the tiller as none of the others were interested in sailing the boat at that point. Once clear of the Calf, Ellis sailed on a course using the north end of Graemsay as his mark. It was a straightforward close reach.

The girls started to discuss what they knew and what they should do next. Hal joined in from time to time, raising his head from the engine compartment where he had taken the carburettor apart and was cleaning it. Ellis listened but did not join in. Partly he simply enjoyed sailing *Solvaig* because it was turning out to be a very pleasant afternoon with a steady breeze, Solvaig's Song appropriately running through his head.

He also wanted to remember exactly what he had heard and seen, ever since his working visit to being on board *Gaia Marina*. When they were about half way home, and the conversation was flagging, Ellis joined in.

"To summarize what you have been saying with what I can remember, we know that there were three plotters, as we called them, behind the screen at the meeting whose conversation I overheard, Grumpy who was on the plane with me, the waiter at the hotel and one other as yet unidentified but his name is Bill. If we add a man called Sid who was to have arrived a week after the meeting that's four. For whatever they plan against the Oil Terminal Grumpy only wanted three men apparently, who must be Grumpy, Bill and Sid. He must be around by now."

"Didn't you say that you had the impression that the plotters were different to those, like Simon, who are now living on Gaia Marina?"

"Yes. When they met behind the screen in the Hall, Grumpy spoke as if briefing the other two. Presumably they knew something of the job, but not the detail. They also said that the six kippers phrase was a password which they no longer needed. They would not have needed a password at all if they had known each other at the start. They must have been employed to carry out some specific job."

"So what about those on the yacht?"

"Malloss who we have just met is probably the leader and is the man Grumpy described as 'the boss'. Beardy, who we met walking when we went to see the YMCA. looks as if he is the Captain of *Gaia Marina*. The third is of course Simon.

*What about Euan and Mark? I can't believe they are in any plot."

"I would guess they are employed to man the yacht and have nothing to do with the plot. *Gaia Marina* is certainly equipped to be worked by just a few crew, if they are reasonably experienced."

"So we have three plotters, not counting the waiter, Grumpy, Bill and Sid. There are two crew, plus a Captain to sail *Gaia Marina*. Then there is Malloss, who must be the 'boss', and the President of PPP according to his new assistant Simon when he spoke to you in the Coffee Pot café.

"But could there not be others we know nothing about?"

"It is certainly a big enough yacht for more crew. But those who had gone with the Captain today could have been Bill and Sid."

"What about the waiter and Andy?"

The waiter seems to be their contact, originally, with Simon. As a Polish waiter, he could be useful and being here temporarily, is unlikely to give anything away. Maybe he has done what he was asked to do and is no longer involved.

Andy acted as if a sort of servant to Malloss. I wonder why he stayed on the yacht rather than help with setting up their play? He was a bit reluctant to help Euan and Mark aboard, perhaps he is not too strong? At least he made them a drink and ensured their bunks were OK. He looked a very unhappy man, as if he had enough to worry about. Even as if he did not want to be there at all."

"So, does that mean there are very few people in the plot, plus a few who are helping?"

"Yes, I can't guess what all this is about but it seems a very small show to do anything to the Oil Terminal."

"But what about Simon? He did not seem to have anything to do on the yacht, but nor had he gone ashore. What is his role in all this, do you think, Ellis?"

"The plotters joking about him, and our distrust, must not lead us to underestimate him. He does seem to have Malloss' ear, and as he worked in admin at the terminal, his knowledge of the terminal security could be useful to the plot. But that may not be his only or even main role. Just to be a spy does not quite fit what we have seen on *Gaia Marina*. For example the way he acted towards us, leaving aside his attitude to Vaila. Malloss asked him to act as host to us, which suggests to me that his job as assistant to PPP's President is not just as a 'gofer' but is something a bit more senior."

"Malloss must have been suspicious of us – why else send the speed boat to see who we were? Yet he didn't ask us why we were sailing towards *Gaia Marina* just now, did he?" Asked Hal.

"Maybe once he learnt that Simon knew us perhaps Malloss decided we were harmless? Or maybe he thought that as Simon knows us, he could keep an eye on what we are up to, and discover our plans and what we knew? He is not to know we have no plans, nor really know much about his plans either, but we must be a puzzle to him because we keep on crossing the path of his people. He can't know it's more by accident than design."

"How much has Simon told him about us?" Asked Inga.

It was Hal who replied, "I bet he told Malloss that Vaila was keen on him, and that you are trying to muscle in, Ellis. But I shouldn't think Malloss would care about Simon's love life, he would only be interested if he thought we'd spoil his plans. There's not much else Simon could have said about us."

"Why doesn't Simon just leave me alone?"

"I'm afraid he's obsessed by you, and jealous of me. That dance incident was the point at which, for you, Simon killed any interest you might have had in him. But he's more concerned that it made him look foolish, it was so public. His reputation as a Casanova was dented, and he felt you humiliated him. That's what he told the waiter. Remember what I overheard behind the screens at the Flotta meeting? It's entirely his own fault of course but I doubt if he sees it that way.

"Then I came on the scene. My guess is that he thought I made things even worse for him. Now he seems to think that I, a boring archeologist is his rival. He can't believe, Vaila, that you wouldn't prefer him, let alone refuse to go out with him at all."

"He doesn't treat you as if he really cares about you Vaila." Said Inga, "He was positively rude to you on *Gaia Marina*."

"He'll still want you to go back to him, just to maintain his pride in being the great lover. Perhaps he is beginning to be afraid he is losing. I hope I am not making the situation worse."

"Of course you are," laughed Inga, "and I'm quite sure Vaila doesn't want you to stop."

Ellis looked at Vaila but she was studying her shoe laces, and when he looked at Inga again she grinned at him. "Vaila and I have been best friends since we were at primary school, she can't hide anything from me!"

Ellis was glad when Hal changed the subject. "What about the money? Didn't he boast to you, Vaila, that he will be very rich quite soon apparently as a result of PPPs activities?"

"That was only talk." She replied.

"Perhaps, but I don't think so. He'd not expect you to believe him for long unless he can prove he has money fairly soon. Perhaps it's a way of saying 'do not commit yourself to Ellis, until my fortune arrives.' I think he genuinely expects to be rich soon."

"But PPP is supposed to be a charity, not a business. Malloss told us that just now. So where does the fortune come from?"

"Yes. Even if PPP has the money to pay Simon a substantial salary, what could Simon do for it that is worth so much? Malloss must regard him as important to their plans. But what has Simon got to offer him?"

"I cannot think of any way he could be useful to any attack on the terminal." said Hal. "He is hardly a man of action. Maybe his local friends are useful, and he can be persuasive, even if not to you, Vaila?"

"There is another puzzle in what I overheard behind the screen at the meeting. Grumpy, As he was briefing the other two, stressed the importance of there being no one hurt and no oil spilt. What an odd thing to say. Why would that occur to a direct action lobby group? Fanatics do not usually worry about folk getting hurt, and if oil pollutes Scapa Flow they would have a good story to back up their anti-pollution campaign, wouldn't they?"

"But would he say that unless what they planned at least risked injury or oil spills?" Asked Inga. "We know that *Gaia Marina* had to go somewhere else to fetch something, so surely their plans cannot be merely to hold a demonstration? What would they need that required the yacht to fetch it?"

"How can three men do much to the terminal anyway?" Mused Ellis. "There are over three hundred employees, the plant is huge and spread out over a very large site, and Simon would have told them that there is a substantial security department. Neither an attack on the terminal, nor Simon's boast that he will get a fortune from PPP appear to make sense. It makes me think that there is something happening apart from the attack on the Terminal."

"Whatever their plans when are they going to do anything?" asked Inga. "It is several weeks since your eavesdropping. Gaia Marina has gone and returned, to anchor in a strange spot. But they do not appear to be doing anything, just waiting."

"Yes and of course they'd expect the terminal to check on them anchored so near. They must have a good story to cover that but why bother? Why anchor in a place that almost invites questions?"

"I can't think of any answers to all those questions. Yet I can't help thinking we have enough clues to work out what is going on. So what are we missing? I have even started to wonder if we are on the wrong track entirely. What if PPP and Malloss aren't planning anything much against the terminal, but have something else in mind altogether, maybe using what appears to be an attack on the terminal as a smoke screen?"

"Malloss invited us to his play tomorrow, perhaps so he could keep tabs on us. He is going nowhere until after that. But he might well want to get on with whatever they plan the day after tomorrow."

"Why don't we go to see Uncle John when we get back to Stromness." Hal suggested, "I agree." Said Ellis. "In any case we should thank him for lending us this beautiful boat to day."

The others were silent for a minute, then Vaila pulled out her mobile, turned it on and checked it. "There is reception even out here so I agree, Ellis. I will ring Uncle John right now." After her call she confirmed that Uncle John would not only be happy to see them, but offered them tea. He had said he would tell Mum that we would be late home.

When they arrived at his house, they were greeted by his wife Sally. She was most welcoming, and already had a substantial tea waiting for them all; "I know sailing makes you hungry." she said. "Not only that but John has hinted that you have had quite an adventure but he has not told me much about it, and on top of that I confess I am longing to meet your new boyfriend, Vaila." Turning to Ellis she continued "I presume you are the archeologist? I have heard a lot about you so it is nice to meet you."

"Yes, that's me, and it is good to meet you too, sorry for the short notice. First, we had a wonderful sail today. *Solvaig* is a beautiful boat and sails really well. Thank you so much for lending her to us."

Hal added, "I think I have repaired the fault in the engine – the carburetor was a bit dirty, and the setting was not quite as I expected, so I adjusted it, and I think it is OK now." Uncle John thanked him.

Ellis laughed "Everywhere I go on Orkney, everyone seems to know who I am. I rather like that, I feel at home, and I like being called Vaila's boyfriend too, not least as she seems happy to be my girlfriend. But am a bit nervous about your verdict of me, Sally! I wonder what you have heard."

"Sally," said Uncle John, "I suggest you leave the poor man alone and reserve your judgment until you have heard their story. What I have heard so far is most interesting. I suggest you tell the whole story up to now. As Sally said, she has heard little of it, and I would like to hear it again. Who will be the story teller?"

"Ellis." Hal, Vaila and Inga instantly agreed.

Ellis replied "Fine, but you can all chip in if I get any of it wrong, or miss bits."

Ellis then recounted their experiences from the moment he first over heard the phrase about the six kippers to their visit to Gaia Marina. He ended with their discussion on *Solvaig* as they sailed home.

He concluded "That is what we have heard, done and seen, but we are still not at all sure what it is all about. We feel we must have most of the facts, but can't draw a clear conclusion from them."

"Ellis, the legal profession has lost out to archeology; that is a wonderfully clear story and an excellent summing up. I am especially intrigued by the suggestion that an attack on the terminal may not be the main objective of Malloss and his PPP. I suggest we do not worry our heads by discussing it all further just now, but if you go to their show tomorrow, I will make some enquiries about Malloss and the others and his charity. How about having dinner together after that? Have I got your mobile number Vaila – and all your numbers? Perhaps you should each have mine too. I agree there is unlikely to be any action for at least two days, but it would be as well if we can keep in touch." They ensured all their phones had all the numbers saved in them.

"Vaila said "Thank you so much Uncle, and Sally thank you for a wonderful tea. We should get back now." She started to get up when she stopped and said to Sally "Magnus and Ellis are always teasing me so this seems a lovely opportunity to get my revenge. Do you think my new boyfriend is good enough for me?"

Sally replied with a wide grin "You will have to watch him very carefully my dear. When this story gets out, half the girls on Orkney will be after him. Don't laugh Inga, the other half will be after Hal!"

Peter and the Wolf.

Hal and Inga, Ellis and Vaila arrived at the hall in good time. In the lobby there was quite a crowd milling around, but they could see through the door into the hall where a number of people were already seated. It looked as if there would be a good audience. The show had been advertised as free, and refreshments were to be included. They were already being served, giving an impression of PPP as a generous organization, and the advertising had certainly encouraged many folk to come to hear about it. Vaila said she wanted to visit the ladies, so Ellis waited for her in the lobby, while Hal and Inga went in ahead to get four seats together.

The waiter and Simon were at the door welcoming the audience and offering free programmes. When Inga and Hal reached him Simon told them how pleased he was to see them and asked. "Have the two of you come alone?"

At that moment he spotted Ellis, apparently by himself in the lobby. "Oh the archeologist is alone – has Vaila fallen out with him?" He sounded hopeful, but Hal soon dashed his hopes, and could not resist the chance to rub it in.

"Oh no, they've just got left behind. I think they are round the corner for a little cuddle!"

Simon smiled "You can't resist pulling my leg can you, I can see Ellis, but she is not with him."

"Ah well, Simon, she must have gone with someone else."

"Very funny; there she is. You go and sit down so I can speak to them uninterrupted."

When Vaila and Ellis reached the door he greeted them as warmly as he could: "I am so glad you have come; PPP is an interesting organization and you can learn a lot from this evening's presentation. My offer of a seat with me at the projection table is still open, Vaila."

"Not tonight, Simon." Vaila started to move into the hall, but Simon stopped her. "Surely you do not need to spend all your time with Ellis. It's not very fair on me. Can you not tear your attention from your temporary boyfriend, just for a little while?"

"I'm sorry Simon, I am with Ellis tonight, temporarily or not," and she walked into the hall. Simon, distracted, watched her join Hal and Inga, so Ellis had to ask for a programme. "Is it better to be temporary or ex? But we are here for the show and you have duties, so you told us."

"When are you going home?" Simon asked as he gave him one.

Ellis did not think Simon really expected an answer, but he said, "At the Flotta meeting you suggested I try harder and offered me hints to improve my social skills. But you should be more relaxed. It is all wrong to see me as a rival in some sort of competition with Vaila as the trophy. She isn't a trophy. She will make her own decisions and if she will not go out with you – or me either - she has every right to be left alone."

"That's all very high minded, Ellis, but you have stolen her from me. Why should I meekly give her up to you? We'll see how you like it when she spurns you for me once you have gone home."

"Simon, as she was never your property I can't steal her, can I? Anyway you told me yourself that you had blotted

118

your copybook with her before she'd met me. You even wanted me to persuade her to go out with you again, but she told you then she would not do so and repeated it on *Gaia Marina*. I am sorry if you are upset by my being with her but that's the way it is. I suggest you accept the situation, for your own good. Otherwise you only look pathetic and get teased. All Vaila asks is that you leave her alone. She does not wish you any harm, and nor do I."

"Oh yes you do. You are reveling in being her temporary boyfriend. I've seen you wheedling your way into her good books. But it won't last. I always get the girls I want; I may have gone too fast at that dance, but I know how to get what I want. Afterwards I just stop going out with them, I don't say good bye in case I have a spare weekend and no one else. But no girl ever rejects me and Vaila won't either once you are out of the way."

"I doubt it. She's far too good for you." Ellis, disgusted by Simon's attitude, turned and walked into the hall, but he heard Simon say under his breath. "Arrogant sod. I'll show you."

Ellis joined the others but, fearing Vaila would not have been happy with his exchange with Simon, just said that Simon had asked when he was going home. He made a mental note to warn her of Simon's threat.

When they were seated, Ellis looked around. The hall in which Peter and the Wolf was being staged was the same one that the meeting concerning the expansion of the Flotta Terminal had been held. On the stage a fairly large silver screen had been set up. Each side of the stage was a loudspeaker and on the right hand side was a chair and lectern. Steps were placed each side to provide easy access from the floor of the hall to the stage. Immediately inside the entrance door there was a pair of tables with two chairs, one either side of the door. A second pair of tables and chairs were set up a little further into the hall, as if making a V shape, which would funnel people past the tables as they were leaving. There were small piles of leaflets and a few pens on each. It was not immediately obvious what these tables were for.

At the back of the hall the projection area to which Simon had referred had been created using two of the large screens, which Ellis recognized; he had seen the plan and heard Grumpy and the plotters through them at the Flotta meeting. Now they were set up with a small gap between them in which a projector was placed.

Hal then suggested they had a bit of fun at Simon's expense – "Vaila, if you took Ellis with you behind those screens, you could really drive Simon crazy – perhaps you could sit on Ellis' knee?"

Ellis laughed, "Very tempting for me, but jealousy is a powerful emotion, and I am beginning to wonder if we are going too far in teasing him. We agreed that he is obsessed by Vaila; would he be crazy enough to do something really rash if we push too hard? I tried to calm him down just now, but to him I am the problem so I was unsuccessful. He can't wait for me to go home.

"I only want him to leave me alone, but do not wish him any harm." Vaila added.

"I told him that."

At that point Malloss came into the hall from a side entrance, which ended their conversation. He crossed to where Simon was still greeting folk as they came in, spoke to him and Simon left the door to the waiter and went to his projection desk behind the screens, whilst Malloss climbed the nearest steps onto the stage. He sat on the chair behind the lectern and checked his script whilst several late comers found seats.

Malloss then stood up and introduced himself as President of PPP, and the first slide came onto the screen, PPP's logo. Ellis and his friends had difficulty not laughing out loud; the logo consisted of six kippers.

"Prevent Pollution on the Planet – PPP for short - is a registered charity. Our logo shows three kippers representing land, water and air, paired with three others skin side up representing threats of waste dumping, pollution of water by our effluent, and air pollution from burning fossil fuels. Why kippers? Only because my wife is fond of them, even If I can't stand them!" He was not good at telling jokes so few folk laughed.

As he continued, the slides illustrated his message. "Our purposes are to work towards a pollution free world. Just think of the benefits for everyone. We all remember those terrible oil spills when the Exxon Valdese went on the rocks in Alaska, the Torrey Canyon on the Scilly Isles or the Braer, just a few miles from here on Fitfull Head in Shetland.

But there are many other forms of pollution that we must eliminate, Industrial air pollution for instance – are you aware that air pollution kills, or contributes to the death of around 16000 people in the UK alone each year? Worse, UK's air pollution has led to acid rain from Scandinavia to Poland? It comes from gases emitted by the use of fossil fuels. It kills trees, which otherwise keep the air we breathe fresh and balanced. What about the Bhopal accident in India – a case of an irresponsible chemical industry killing hundreds of people through accidental, but careless emissions? It goes much further than that; the terrible problems arising from Nuclear Power stations when something goes wrong – Chernobyl and Three Mile Island are examples of how accidents alone can pollute large areas. I could go on and on, but I am sure you understand the major threats that we face of which the cases I mentioned are a few examples. But there are small threats too. We must not forget the problems from small escapes of horrible wastes into the sea, from landfill sites, from factories careless of their wastes. There is a suspicion that even these apparently small polluting activities may be poisoning underground water aquafers. What is that doing to our health?

"Do not assume that you are free of such problems here on Orkney. Within a few miles you have a nuclear facility, and a major oil terminal. You have land fill sites too. Besides, Orkney is part of Britain, and you and your families travel do they not? You use fossil fuels, you visit places full of smoke, grime and polluted water, probably unaware of the poisons they produce.

"What is so much worse is that the main victims from such events are not only ourselves, but our children and grandchildren – do you really want to leave a dirty planet as your legacy to them? What about the animals for whom we are learning to give greater respect? None of the pollution is their fault, but they suffer none the less.

"So how are we to do something about it? When we formed PPP we thought hard about how we could help clean up our planet. We decided on three areas where we believe we could make a difference. First we should advertise and inform – that is what we are doing this evening of course.

Second we should lobby our Government, and eventually on a larger scale at the EU and UN. Third we should provide small demonstrations of intent, through direct action. Nothing unethical, and certainly nothing that would hurt anyone or – heaven forbid - causes pollution itself. We do not want to prevent industry functioning either, after all some companies show exemplary responsibility, but accidents will happen. So even if we feel, for example, that the company running the Flotta terminal are amongst the good guys, what they are doing is still risky. We cannot relax our vigilance, but must take every opportunity to help them avoid accidents and follow the best practice. We must take action to wake them up to our presence. If we ensure our actions cost them money and reputation, they will take notice of PPP and our cause.

"It is of course a giant task, which we are attempting with the minimum of resources. We do not have an office to maintain for example, and I personally have donated my private yacht to PPP, as a mobile base. You may have seen her in Scapa Flow; a ketch with a green hull called *Gaia Marina*. We gave her that name, to illustrate what we were about. Gaia is mother earth in some legends, and marina is of course of the sea. Much better than her previous name of *Ocean Rider*. She enables us to travel under sail so we use the minimum of the earth's resources. She is currently anchored by the Calf of Golta. From our anchorage we can keep an eye on what happens at the terminal, how carefully the tanker operation is carried out and so on. It is not a comfortable place to anchor, and it makes it difficult to come ashore but we do not mind as we are dedicated to the cause.

"But those of us dedicated to PPP cannot manage on our own. We are in talks with the largest of the non-Governmental conservation organizations such as the National Trust for Scotland and the National Trust, RSPB etc. If we can achieve a united campaign, then the influence we will wield will surely be decisive.

"This is where you can help the cause. Donations are important, but we hope you will want to help for the longer term by becoming a member. I suppose we could have added another 'P' to our title to stand for 'people', indicating how important each and every one of you are to this important work, but it is actions that sound louder than words. A large membership means that those in power, the politicians, will listen to our message. As a non-government conservation body, we do not claim to be powerful, but, backed by a growing membership, we will become more influential, and it is yourselves, as members of PPP, that will get the credit for the success of this valuable work. That is why we particularly hope you will be persuaded to join this evening.

"To help make our work memorable we will now play the well-known folk tale of Peter and the Wolf. In your programme is our interpretation of the story for the twenty first century; we hope you will enjoy the story and music, and that it will, for each of you become the anthem of our cause - PPPs noble mission statement. We want PPP to belong to its members – so that "we" comes to mean you all. An organization that will catch the 'wolf' – the polluters."

"On your programme is a synopsis of the story in the left hand column and our interpretation on the right.

"The Programme also includes an application form to join PPP, and as you leave some of our staff and volunteers

124

will gladly help you complete the form. Thank you very much for coming. There are plenty more refreshments for you to enjoy."

Malloss then sat down, and Simon and the waiter took their places at the tables by the door. Two other men also came forward to sit at the remaining two tables.

"What did you make of that?" asked Inga.

"It sounded good." said Hal "but why do I feel suspicious of Malloss?"

Vaila responded "It's no good asking me, I am concentrating on avoiding Simon! Tell me, am I being paranoid about him? I managed all right on my own in the café a few weeks ago, and surely he will soon have to accept that all I want him to do is to leave me alone. But somehow I feel more and more uneasy about him each time we meet."

Ellis said "No, Vaila, you are not being paranoid. Maybe irritated by his refusal to take no for an answer, and properly careful. To us he is making a fool of himself. To you his obsession is bound to be a bit daunting. You must wonder what he will do next. You are right to try to avoid him."

"Orkney is a small place, I am bound to bump into him from time to time. It is a bit more than irritation, I am getting nervous about him."

Hal said "I certainly think you are right to be cautious. But what can he do? If he is that keen on you he would not hurt you."

Ellis was not sure he agreed with that, but he did not want to increase Vaila's anxiety by saying anything. He was beginning to worry about what would happen when he had to go back to work in Inverness, but could not think of anything he could do to help her. At least Hal would be there to support her.

Hal suggested they go home so they made for the door.

To get out they had to make their way through the small crowd around the door. Simon, the Waiter and the other staff were talking to as many as they could urging them to sign up as members of PPP. Malloss was also talking to them, acting rather like a politician seeking votes. He spotted Ellis and his friends, came up to them, "I am so glad you came. Did you enjoy the show? Did it interest you in PPP? I do hope you will join."

Ellis said "Oh we were wondering how much you would be able to do with a mere £2 subscription?"

"Good management is the key. The lobbying, for example is something that is done on a one to one basis – I will do most of it myself, so the costs are negligible. Are you going to join? I am sure Simon would be delighted to process your application."

It was Vaila who answered that question. "Not tonight, he is busy with other folk just now and he would be disappointed if someone else looked after me. He's even jealous of my coming tonight with my brother and my friends! Good evening Sir Frank." And she left the hall before Malloss could say any more. Ellis smiled at Malloss, and also wished him goodnight; Hal and Inga followed them out of the hall. Malloss looked as if he was going to say more, but there were a lot of people around him who he wanted to encourage to join. But his glance at Vaila as she left the hall was not friendly. He seemed to Ellis a man that did not expect or tolerate anyone walking out on him.

Prevent Planet Pollution

Presents its interpretation for the modern world

Of

Peter and the Wolf.

A folk tale with music by Prokofiev

PPP plays Peter (Strings)

The Government plays Grandpa (Bassoon)

People are played by the bird (Flute) and the duck. (Oboe)

Animals are represented by the Cat (Clarinet)

The polluters are played by the wolf (Horns.)

Global organizations are The Hunters (timpani)

Peter is at home. He wants to play in the meadow, although the gate is closed.

But Peter opens the gate.

Encouraged by a bird singing to him, 'Come on Peter.'

He goes into the meadow to hunt the wolf.

Then a duck comes into the meadow.

The bird flies down and says to the duck "You are a silly bird. Can you not fly into the tree?

The duck says you are the silly one – what sort of bird cannot swim?

The Bird and the duck argue and argue forgetting the dangers of the meadow.

The cat comes into the meadow and stalks the birds while they argue.

Peter shouts "look out!"

The bird flies into the tree and the duck swims to the centre of the pond.

PPP is ready to start work, but has few resources, & faces Government and commerce holding PPP back. But PPP is determined, and starts work.
Supporters encourage PPP

First PPP sets out its case to MPs in London and MSPs in Edinburgh.

Word spreads. Others want to join.

But some argue for their own cause alone.
They forget the dangers pollution pose to both animal and human life.

Arguments encourage others to emphasize differences.

Arguments pose danger to the cause

PPP sees the necessity of conservation bodies working together. e.g. PPP supports Animal rights, which are important, and need promotion but there is a danger that the PPPs message is diluted, unless all causes unite, with a single theme; all creatures suffer pollution.

Peter is called back by his Grandpa – for safety reasons. Boys do not hunt wolves they are dangerous.

The wolf comes quietly out of the forest into the meadow.

The bird, duck and cat see the wolf – the cat joins the bird in the Tree - on a different branch -

The duck jumps out of the water and tries to run away. The wolf chases her, but she is not fast enough. The wolf catches her and swallows her whole.

He walks round and round the tree, unable to reach the bird and cat.

Peter sees the wolf and fetches a length of rope. He runs to the tree when the wolf is not looking & climbs up. Peter makes a loop in the rope, and tells the bird to fly round the wolf to distract it.

Peter catches the wolf with his rope. The Hunters come and the wolf is led away.

Pollution can be dangerous, but PPP will not be stopped by petty health and laws safety.

Pollution can be quiet and subtle

PPP persuades most to work together in a campaign and direct action. It does not detract from each NGOs cause, but confuses the polluter

But those who will not join the joint effort risk losing everything.

PPP devises ways to catch out the polluters and is prepared to take risks

PPP's campaign is successful. Pollution is cleaned up. The polluters suffer the punishment the law requires.

Here is how you can help. Please take this opportunity to join PPP and show how much you care. It only costs £2!!!

APPLICATION TO JOIN PPP.

Full name   ....

Address   ....

.......…................... Post code ....

E mail   ....

Phone number.................................... Mobile   phone   number ....

Please help us by ticking the following boxes if they apply;

Are you a member of; Treasures of Scotland O; National Trust for Scotland O;

RSPB O; Scottish Wildlife Trust O; Marine Conservation Society O; Woodland Trust   O If you would like our free newsletter half yearly we will need to retain your details. If not please write or ring to tell us, otherwise we will send it to you.

I enclose a cheque/cash to PPP as my subscription for a year   £ 2

Plus a donation of   £

Total   £

Gift Aid; as a taxpayer if you agree to do so, we can claim the tax back on your contribution – it costs you nothing! Just sign once as this is a continuing agreement

Signature...

Date.......................

THANK YOU VERY MUCH FOR JOINING

Gaia Marina box 5673, Mail Service Company. Invern

Flotta again

As they walked home from Peter and the Wolf they discussed it further. Ellis asked "Would you join PPP on the basis of what Malloss had to say? Do you think anyone else you know well would do so?"

To which Hal replied, "I will not join, and doubt if any of my friends or family would either. The cause sounds a good one, but I just do not like Malloss, nor especially his new assistant."

"Malloss is a powerful man, and persuasive but I could not trust him. He seems only interested in himself, and I wonder why a man like that would ever do anything charitable – anything for anyone but himself?"

Hal continued, "Inga, to change the subject what shift are you on tomorrow?"

"Mornings, officially but this week we are a bit short staffed due to holidays, so I doubt if I will be home until late afternoon."

"Well, I am working tomorrow so I'll ring you on the way home. Let's go out in the evening – something a bit more fun than listening to Malloss. Why don't you come in now for a coffee with us? Then I'll take you home in the car."

As they were making coffee the phone rang. Ellis picked it up; it was Magnus.

"Sorry both to ring so late and to spoil your holiday but I thought you might be interested in taking another photo of the YMCA site on Flotta. HQ want another, as the one you took earlier was not very clear due to the haa. You have a permit to go there and it would certainly save me a lot of hassle. It's you after all that has abducted my secretary – she promised to help me whilst I'm all alone here in the office. No doubt she is with you."

"That's OK," said Ellis, "I know how you suffer! I'll tell Vaila. I will take my local guide with me, I wouldn't like you to abduct her back!"

"You are getting to know me too well young man! Many thanks. You can go back to cuddling her now!" With a quick chuckle he rang off before Ellis could think of a suitable reply.

After explaining to Hal and Vaila what Magnus had asked, without his final remark, Ellis suggested they went over on the early morning ferry to make the most of the day.

"Would you be free to join us, Hal?" Ellis asked. "We might get a good view of Gaia Marina from the YMCA site. I could take you in my car to Houton this time."

"Yes. I need to look at the perimeter fence on the east side anyway, and many thanks for the offer of a lift too. I have an uneasy feeling about that east fence. I might as well see it tomorrow morning. Don't forget to bring your passes. I will deal with the office, although as Triscoll himself said you were to be given free access, that's even better than a pass."

The next day the three of them took the ferry to Flotta, chose a bike each from the company shed and set off on the Golta road. The weather was dry but cloudy and reasonably warm so they talked as they rode. At the point that the road did a wide s bend soon after passing through the terminal tank farm, Hal pointed out the scrub woodland between the road and perimeter fence, one of the scraps of woodland left from an attempt to plant woods on Flotta after the war.

"That's the reason I keep a close watch on the east fence; it is difficult to see what goes on in that scrub and if ever an attack was made on the terminal, this must be the sort of place the perpetrators might choose to get through the fence unseen. I am waiting for contractors to come to clear this area but they cannot come until next month."

As soon as they got to the YMCA, Ellis said "I'll just take the photos. See what you can of Gaia Marina while I do that – and Vaila, don't climb on the wall!" Vaila laughed.

"What's the joke?" asked Hal, but Vaila told him with a giggle that it was a secret.

"Oh I see. You two have secrets now do you. I will have to get Inga to apply some suitable medical torture – she must know ways to make you talk!"

Having taken the photos from the front and within the foundation walls, including the large chimney, Ellis joined Hal and Vaila watching Gaia Marina, anchored by the Calf of Golta still in the same anchorage in which she had been when they had rescued the two men from the speed boat accident.

There were few signs of life on the yacht but Hal pointed to a dinghy tied up at the end of the road beside the St Vincent pier. "Someone must have landed from Gaia Marina."

"I can't see anyone though, all seems quiet." said Vaila. She thought she caught sight of movement towards the rocket battery site, but dismissed it as a rabbit, without mentioning it to the others.

"Yes that's odd," said Ellis "someone must have come ashore – several people could have come in that large dinghy. They must be somewhere on the peninsula."

"There is only the beach at Roan head. I cannot imagine what would be of interest there. We can see most of the rest of the ground and I still think we would see them if they were close by. Could they have got to the scrub woodland just after the tank farm before we rode passed it?" questioned Hal. "We should ride back and this time concentrate on looking very carefully for anyone moving about. Ellis, you look on the south side of the road, I will look on the north and Vaila you ride a couple of meters or so ahead to watch the road. Ride quite slowly so we can look properly. If we see nothing before we get to the nearest point to the east perimeter fence, we'll check it, and then return to the office to see if any other permits have been issued today."

They saw nothing exceptional until they arrived at the point from which Hal wanted to check the fence. As soon as they stopped they heard someone talking beyond a small hillock or ridge - shaped rather like a small long barrow, thought Ellis. It was no more than three meters high and beyond it, especially to the right from where they were, the shrub seemed especially thick. Leaving the bikes Hal and Ellis quickly scrambled up to the top of it.

They found themselves over looking two men working at something on the fence.

One wore an overall. He was not especially tall, but was thick set, with a pugilist's face, it looked as if his nose might have been broken sometime in the past. The other was a little taller, with a mean, narrow face, who wore, of all things, a sports jacket, although it looked as if it had seen better days. Apparently supervising them was a third man, immediately recognizable as Grumpy.

Hal called out "What are you doing? You have no business touching the fence!"

The men working on the fence stopped and looked at them in surprise. Clearly they did not welcome Hal's call. Grumpy told the men to get back to work and said "We have permits to be here." As he said this Hal ran down the slope. Ellis realizing they were outnumbered said to Vaila, who had stayed at the bottom of the hillock, "Quickly, go back to the road and ring for help on your mobile. If you do not have the number in your phone, use the number on your pass. When security come you will need to guide them here as they will not see where we are from the road. It is as well you keep out of sight. Quickly now."

Vaila ran back as he had asked her. Ellis turned back to see Hal talking to Mr. Grumpy very firmly.

" I am in charge of the maintenance of this fence, and have not ordered work on it. So stop at once and come with me to the office."

"Oh really," said Grumpy in a cynical and threatening voice. "I don't care who you are. You are interfering in what we are doing and I cannot have that. Sid and Bill – sort this silly man out."

"What about him?" said Sid, the taller of the men, pointing to Ellis who was now running down the slope.

"Sort them both – it should not be beyond you two. They both look like office types."

Sid took a sudden lunge at Hal that caught him off balance and he fell. Ellis joined in, pushing Sid back, but was attacked by Bill. Hal scrambled to his feet and hit Sid, but the blow was warded off. Sid took a step back, put his hand in his pocket and pulled out a knife.

"They've got knives" warned Hal. Ellis, distracted by Hal's call, failed to dodge Bills fist as it swung at him. He staggered back dazed, but he kept on his feet. He saw that Bill did not seem to have a knife. He recovered to see Hal backing before Sid triumphantly swinging his knife at him.

"No knives, the boss said" called Grumpy.

"Sod that, I don't like being interrupted in my work by bloody silly boys."

Bill however paused which enabled Ellis, seeing Hal in danger from Sid's knife, to run at Sid and hit him hard. He immediately turned round to meet Bill. He turned so quickly that Bill's attempt to hit him, missed. Ellis took the opportunity to hit him whilst he was off balance.

It did little harm to Bill, just made him pause long enough for Ellis to see Sid, furious at being surprised, take his revenge by a vicious stab with his knife at Hals left arm held up in defence.

Hal cried out in pain, as Sid pushed him roughly to the ground.

At this Grumpy intervened. "Stop that. We don't need it."

As Ellis had his back to him, Grumpy grabbed Ellis from behind, pushing his arms up his back in a half nelson.

"Bill, get the rope; tie this one up."

Ellis protested that Hal was in considerable pain, his arm was covered in blood, and was bleeding profusely.

"For goodness sake let me attend to him. He'll not fight further, and there's nothing I can do against three of you."

"OK, no talking and no interference with our work." Grumpy replied.

Turning to Sid, "Stay near them and for once you can keep that knife ready, in case he gets difficult. I am still not sure who he really is, but I do know he's the damned archeologist who keeps interfering. He can't do us much harm. I'll join Bill in completing the job."

He then walked back to the fence with Bill and started to get things from the rucksack lying on the ground.

Ellis knelt beside Hal who smiled weakly, and mouthed a silent "Sorry."

Ellis mouthed back "Vaila will have phoned by now."

"Shut up, or you'll f'ing get it." Growled Sid.

Ellis started to work out where Hal had been slashed, and how badly. He worked slowly, to avoid giving Sid any excuse to use the knife again, and of course, to ensure he did not hurt Hal further. But he had hardly started when he was horrified to see Vaila come over the hillock, her wrist held in Simon's firm grip.

Simon shouted. "Here we are. Sorry I am a bit late. I had no sooner done the little job at the pier for the boss, when I saw this lot at the ruin. I managed to hide behind the big chimney and to hear and see what they were up to, I heard them discussing where you might be, and when I saw

137

where they were going I followed them. They got ahead of me on bikes, of course, but I arrived here just in time to stop the girl trying to phone for help."

"Who is she?" asked Grumpy. Vaila, slipped out of Simons grip on her arm and ran to Hal lying on the ground, before Simon could reply. Regardless of Sid, Ellis told her what had happened.

"Let me see what I can do. – Who did this?"

Ellis replied, nodding at the assailant, "Sid is the one with the knife."

"And I'll do it to you too, you daft bugger, if you don't shut up."

Vaila stood up, turned to Sid and said with venom in her voice.

"Bastard; you should end in jail for this, and you will."

Putting on a mocking childlike voice Sid said "Oh dear I'm terrified." Bill joined in the same voice "Sidney dear, I think you've hurt the poor little girl's boyfriend, perhaps you should say sorry please to them."

Grumpy intervened, "That's enough we have serious business to complete."

To Simon he said "That man," pointing to Ellis, "seems to be an archaeologist but I'm beginning to wonder. He was on my plane several weeks ago. He knew the password, Stanis said he used it to him in the hotel. I thought he'd gone. Now he's here with his friends. Presumably they are the ones you said came to the boat, and you knew them. So answer my question, who are they?"

Simon smiled, enjoying the moment. "Oh yes, you didn't see them on *Gaia Marina*, did you. The man on the ground is Harold Flett, he likes to be called Hal and to think he is a good maintenance surveyor. He is not so hot with engines either. The girl is his sister; but Sid can be forgiven calling him her boyfriend because they have a strangely cozy relationship – incestuous if you ask me. Do you not remember my telling you about them? She wanted to be my girlfriend at one time, but I dumped her when she got boring.

"But then the prize of the bunch" – he pointed at Ellis – "the archeologist is Ellis MacKenzie who thought he would take the girl for himself, the self-righteous sod. She fell for it, she is easily flattered, but I do believe she will shortly change her mind; I have pleasant ideas for her and unpleasant ones for him." He smiled round the others in triumph. "We cannot let them go telling tales to the security people so I suggest we take them as our prisoners back to the yacht to avoid them causing us any more inconvenience. Malloss will know what to do with the boys, and I know what to do with the girl!"

Ellis thought there was a touch of madness in Simon's voice and he was obviously delighted with the situation. Ellis tried to remain calm himself, not least to enable him to think clearly. He just said in a quiet but hard voice "So, Simon, are you so weak that you have to get these others to do your dirty work? I am surprised, Sid, that you allow this creep to give you orders."

Grumpy said very firmly "Shut up all of you, enough nonsense. Bill tie MacKenzie's hands like I told you to. I do not think we will have much trouble from the one you knifed, Sid. Simon, seeing you are so fond of the girl, you deal with her. I suggest you do not get sentimental with her until we are aboard."

"Thank you, I would be delighted to look after her.

Come on now Vaila, this is no time to make trouble." He took her arm, but she angrily shook it free, and knelt again to do what she could for Hal. Grumpy continued, "Bill and I will complete this job. Sid and Simon, watch our prisoners."

It did not take long. Ellis, watching saw that they were attaching a small amount of what he presumed were explosives to one of the fence posts, and then set a timer. He wondered how long the fuse was but felt it must be at least long enough for them to get back to the yacht - possibly a lot longer. He did not think there was much chance of it being discovered unless he could send a message. To phone or text with his hands tied was impossible. He felt he would have little chance of doing so in any event at that moment, but wondered if there might be an opportunity a bit later.

Grumpy seemed to read his thoughts, because as soon as he was satisfied that their little bomb was properly set, he told Bill and Sid to search Hall and Ellis for mobile phones. They quickly found and removed their mobiles and threw them into the undergrowth, and helped themselves to the money they found. Simon said he had already removed Vaila's phone. Ellis wondered what he had done with it.

The three of them were then marched to the St Vincent pier, Sid walking behind them holding his knife ready in case they tried anything. At least, now they were walking, Ellis' hands were freed. Vaila walked with Hal, Ellis walked on Hal's other side, beside his wounded arm, mainly to ensure no one else did, and also to talk to him, to keep his spirits up. Simon who was obviously enjoying the situation, walked by Vaila. She ignored him, except when he tried to hold her arm, when she shook him off.

Only Ellis would have had any chance of escaping, but he would not desert Hal and Vaila. Grumpy clearly intended to forestall even that remote chance, and walked with Bill a couple of metres behind Sid so that he would see, and could act on any move Ellis made.

Hal was clearly in pain, and Vaila walking beside him looked anxious for him. Ellis hoped Hal would keep going and wondered if there would be a good first aid kit on *Gaia Marina*.

The dinghy tied up next to the St Vincent pier was large enough for all of them. Grumpy, Bill and an entirely unrepentant Sid watched, without making any attempt to assist, as Hal was helped by Ellis and Vaila into it, and once they were all aboard Grumpy started the outboard and they returned to Gaia Marina through the narrow channel available for boats between Golta and the Calf.

When they were alongside *Gaia Marina* Bill and Sid immediately climbed up on to the yacht and secured the lines. Again Ellis and Vaila were left to get Hal aboard. Grumpy remained in the dinghy by the outboard, to ensure they did not take the dinghy. It proved difficult for Hal to climb aboard as he could not use his left arm to hold on to anything to help him climb up.

Ellis suggested Vaila go up first. He then stood behind to help and to ensure Hal did not fall. In this way Hal got onto the deck, Simon just watched, getting in the way in his determination to stay close to Vaila. Ellis was concerned for Hal's injury as there seemed little hope of anyone giving him the attention he needed but he was also full of admiration for Hal's determination not to give way to the pain.

Getting Hal on board at least enabled Vaila to tell Simon to stand back and to stop trying to hold her arm so she could help him. Simon accepted the situation, with a sour comment about how charming it was to see little sister helping her protector, and was gratified that Bill, who was also watching after securing the stern line, at least laughed.

Once on board they were taken to the cockpit; this time not for drinks and a chat, but, as Beardy, the Captain said, so the crew could watch them as they got the yacht ready for sea. Ellis asked him for the first aid kit so that they could make Hal more comfortable, but the Captain ignored the request. The rest of the crew who had come aboard with them went forward to the fore hatch and to their accommodation below as soon as the prisoners were seated in the cockpit, and Simon remained in the cockpit enjoying the success he had had to capture them.

Malloss appeared briefly, equally ignoring them. He made it clear to Simon that he was not happy at having any prisoners aboard.

He then turned to the Captain and said, "Raise the anchor and set a course south out of Scapa Flow, and as soon as we are in the Pentland Firth, turn eastwards. I had intended to sail straight to our home port, but these prisoners are a complication I must deal with. Once you have given your orders, we will sort out what to do about them. Come to the saloon, and you too Simon. They cannot escape."

"Yes, Sir." Replied Beardy – Ellis still did not know his proper name – "I think we should continue under engine until well clear of the land. There's not much wind just now."

"Very well. I will be back shortly." Malloss went below.

The Captain addressed the helmsman who sat at the wheel and back to the cockpit where Vaila, Hal and Ellis sat.

"Once clear of Roan Head, steer due south. We will then round Brough Ness, onto 095^0, north of Muckle Skerry Light and out into the North Sea. Remain as far from shore as reasonable. As you heard, I intend to stay on engine, but call me if the wind gets up. Call me anyway as soon as we have Brough Ness abeam or if this lot are a problem. Keep a sharp lookout for other shipping, especially the Pentland ferry. They steam as if they own these waters; perhaps they do!" He laughed, as he too went below.

Gaia Marina again.

When they had come aboard from *Solvaig* Ellis had had his mind on other things. He had certainly paused to admire *Gaia Marina*, but that was quite different. Now he looked around for inspiration as to how they could escape.

There was a small stern cabin. The cockpit where they sat was about 4 meters fore and aft, and the full beam of the yacht, about the same, so that it was roughly square. During their previous visit there had been comfortable cushions on the fixed seats against the port and starboard sides, which had been removed. At the forward end of the cockpit was the covered steering position, which the Captain called the wheel house. It had a fixed windscreen, the full beam of the yacht, with solid screens to port and starboard both with large windows. It was open to the cockpit, again the full width of the yacht. There were fixings for a canvas screen to enclose it in bad weather, but these were not in place so Ellis saw the helmsman in his high seat, back to them. That he had already taken his seat indicated that the yacht was nearly ready to sail. In front of him was a surprisingly small wheel and below the windscreen either side of the wheel were a number of instruments and switches, including the engine controls. At the port side of the steering position was the hatch, looking like a pair of small outward opening double doors with a small porthole in each to give light to the accommodation below deck. On the starboard side were several lockers.

The hatch was closed so, frustratingly for Ellis, he was unable able to see beyond the hatch doors. Presumably, he thought, there would be a couple of steps down, probably leading to a saloon and dining area.

Nor could he see what was happening on the deck forward, unless he stood up, because the windscreen was too high. He did not want to upset their captors until he had worked out what they could do, so stayed where he was.

Vaila sat by Hal, trying to make him more comfortable and was able to tie something round the injured arm to protect the wound and put his wrist between the buttons of his shirt as a makeshift sling. Ellis was on her other side.

Speaking in a whisper so that the helmsman did not hear, Ellis asked "Vaila, Grumpy & co took our mobiles, but did Simon take yours or have you still got it?"

"The idiot told me to drop it, I had no choice, and dropped it into a clump of grass. But when I tried to dodge him, I tripped. I landed right by it, so I grabbed it again before he dragged me up. He was so full of having captured me that he even tried to kiss me; I let him, which so distracted him that he never noticed my slipping it into my pocket! Since then I'd forgotten about it." She pulled it out.

"Have you got reception?"

"Yes, but weak. Not much battery charge left either. I forgot to turn it off."

"Then I suggest you text Uncle John. How about 'SOS held on GM in Firth. Bomb on east fence. SOS V' ?"

When she had written and sent it Ellis asked "Any charge left?" "Not much, both reception and charge show only one bar.

"Try phoning if only to say 'Check text now.'"

She did as he asked but said, "No, the phone has gone dead. I just hope the text went through. I do not know if Uncle John checks his mobile much."

Ellis replied, "Then we must assume we are on our own."

Shortly afterwards Gaia Marina got underway, and shortly after that Malloss, Grumpy and Simon came through the hatch.

Malloss said "It's a pity we are put to the inconvenience of having you on board, and I am sure you will come to regret it too. If only you had not interfered, and been such a serious nuisance to me.

Mr Grady has told me what happened on shore. (He nodded to the man they knew as Grumpy). He was at fault too by allowing you to see what he was doing.

"As I explained at our 'Peter and the Wolf' show, we do give little samples of direct action, carefully avoiding injury or pollution of any kind because they put donors off. A hole in the fence would have sufficed and, by itself, is not something I need hide, as the blame rightly falls on those that did it, if they are identified."

Grady looked at Malloss with an expression that confirmed his nickname. He was clearly angry at the thought that Malloss might pin all the blame on him should they be caught.

"The problem I face is that I cannot be sure of what you know," continued Malloss, "but whatever it is, it appears to be too much. I cannot trust anything you say to me or that you would remain silent about whatever you know if I just

146

put you ashore. I have to ensure you cannot be a danger to us. So I have decided to offer you a choice.

"The first option would be for you to join us, to be part of PPP. I expect our work to produce considerable profit, so it would be a profitable option for you too. But you must be clear about what I would expect of you. First, a real and absolute guarantee so you could not change your minds.

"This will be partly achieved, Mr Flett and Mr MacKenzie, by you both signing a contract that will make it clear that you have willingly joined PPP and accept full responsibility as part of all it does – including this morning's bomb if necessary." (Grady looked a little relieved) "You will, of course, answer to me as the President and Director General. I expect all our employees to obey my orders without question. You will not be based in Orkney, but in some of Britain's larger cities. You will not have the option to resign or even leave that city, and of course you will be separated. It is a lifetime contract. In short your membership of PPP must be irreversible.

"To be absolutely sure you will not renege on the contract I intend one other thing to ensure your loyalty. I require Miss Flett to marry Simon."

Ellis felt her recoil in horror and he put his hand on her arm and very quietly said "Let him finish, this is not the moment."

Malloss continued, "Simon tells me you are fond of each other."

Vaila could not contain herself "Rubbish".

Malloss turned to her and replied harshly "Keep quiet, listen,"

"As I was saying. Simon also tells me that you, Mr Flett, have an unnaturally close relationship to your sister and object to Simon.

"As far as you are concerned Mr MacKenzie, Simon described to me your boast to him that it would be an amusing holiday challenge, to play on her weaknesses, the weaknesses all women have, to fool her into falling for you which Simon found irritating. Simon doubts that you will admit it in her presence, but believes you would be happy to forget her, if encouraged by a bonus of, say £25000. A good bargain, I'd say, to abandon a light holiday romance."

It was Ellis' turn to say "Nonsense."

Malloss ignored him, and continued. "History is full of powerful people cementing their alliances through marriage, and it is an excellent way to ensure you each become part of our plans on a permanent basis. So, Miss Flett you will marry Simon as soon as we are in international waters, in a ceremony performed by the Captain who, of course, has the traditional right to do so."

Simon added, speaking to Vaila, "Isn't that a wonderful idea? To be married at sea this afternoon. I do hope the weather is fine. So romantic, and we can honeymoon in my nice cosy cabin. I am sure you'll enjoy it my dearest."

Ellis thought Vaila would explode with fury, "I will never ever marry you. Leave me alone."

Malloss interjected in a frightening, yet quiet voice, "You will do what you are told. Did I not tell you I expected obedience? Anyway it is for the men to decide, I am not interested in the opinion of a silly girl, so keep quiet."

"How dare you try to force that man on my sister. I will never abandon her. Nor is my loyalty to her the slightest unnatural. Simon has no sister or he might not be so stupid. I remain totally opposed because she is. You have no right whatsoever to demand any such thing"

"Even if you are so misguided to continue your objection, what are you going to do about it with that arm? It is you that is stupid."

Ellis looked Malloss in the eye. He said steadily, matching Malloss' quietly spoken delivery, but in his case with the purpose of ensuring Malloss could not doubt his resolution, "I too will object in the strongest terms. Simon is lying anyway.

"Vaila told Simon she disliked him well before she even met me and I made no boast such as he has described to you. Hal and Vaila are well aware of that. We will never accept such a medieval idea. I strongly object to any illegal forced marriage to a man she has rejected. She has made her decision clear and that is that. Simon's insane jealousy led him to tell you a pack of lies. He will let you down too sooner or later. He has already given away a lot of your plans"

Malloss, still in a soft voice, but now with increasing menace, replied. "I am afraid I trust Simon more than you. I repeat, the girl will do as she is told.

"However, I said that you would have a choice. If you refuse my offer you will leave us as soon as we are in the Pentland Firth. You can jump, or be thrown off Gaia Marina into the sea and swim ashore, about two or three miles away, if you can. Do not even think we will be blamed for your death, should you fail. I can easily cover that contingency. Your bodies will show no marks apart from the cut in Mr Flett's arm, and no one will know how he got that after he has been in the water for a day or two.

"You would have to go a little later, Miss Flett, as you must be punished for the way you speak to me. You will entertain Sid and Bill before your swim.

"It's up to you, MacKenzie and Flett. I will now leave you for, say an hour, to think it over while we have lunch. By that time we will be conveniently in the Pentland Firth."

There was a short silence when Malloss, Simon and Grumpy went below. Ellis put his arm round Vaila and with Hal on the other side of her, he hoped they were some comfort.

She said, with sheer misery on her face and in her voice. "I suppose I'll have to marry him; it's the only way."

"No my darling, it is a trick" said Ellis. "Maloss will never let us go because he thinks we know all his plans. I suspect we certainly know enough to frustrate them. Simon probably thought up the marriage idea for his own gratification, and Malloss may have agreed just to keep us quiet for a while. Clearly Malloss does not understand loyalty or love. As Hal said, we will not abandon you Vaila, even for a moment, let alone have you suffer at the hands of his goons. As long as I have breath it will not happen.

He also wants us to sign his so-called contract. A written confession that we planted the bomb would help him no end. Once he has got rid of us, we would not be there to say that we were forced to sign."

"I agree with Ellis, it is a trick. I cannot see how option one could work. How will he know what we would do when away from him? He must know that forced marriages are

150

illegal, and therefore invalid. He surely hopes we will reject option one and intends to kill us by throwing us overboard. The 'choice' is to keep us quiet until we are out at sea."

Vaila turned to Ellis and Hal. "If we must die please take me with you. It would be some comfort to know I will be with you."

"My darling we are not beaten yet. Let's concentrate on getting out of this. We must find a way. There must be one."

Neither Malloss and his colleagues, nor the three of them had taken much notice of the helmsman, who had been on watch sitting on the high seat and back to them ever since they were brought on board, hardly an hour previously. But now they saw him checking if anyone was on deck. He left his seat and quietly ensured the hatch was properly shut. He picked up the phone, pressed a button and said "Mark, you are on the next watch, but please come up now. Say nothing, just do it."

He put down the phone and turned round and said, "I am sure you will recognize me – Euan. You rescued Mark and me from the speed boat. Everyone forgets the helmsman but we can hear most of what is said. I'm horrified by what Malloss threatens you with and Mark will be too."

When Mark arrived, as with all the crew, from the fore hatch and along the deck, Euan put him in the picture and explained to Ellis, Vaila and Hal that they were the professional crew hired to sail Gaia Marina.

"We have nothing to do with Malloss, Simon and the rest. The Captain is in whatever it is too. Andy is cook and general dogsbody, and I don't know what he thinks, but he is scared stiff of Malloss, and hardly speaks to anyone. We thought there was something fishy about this trip but didn't expect maniacs like Malloss and Simon. We just do our jobs as the pay is good. We promised we would help you if you needed it, and this is obviously the time you do. I'm sorry you even had to hear what he said, Vaila."

She smiled at him.

Ellis had been looking around as Euan spoke, and then asked,

"Thank you, we definitely need help. I have an idea. Can I borrow the binoculars?"

He had a quick look about 45° off the port bow though the windscreen, and again over the port side of the cockpit without the screen intervening.

He turned to Euan and Mark "I expect you have sailed through to the Pentland Firth this way many times. Would you recognize the Pentland ferry? There is a ship coming this way over there, still hull down from here."

He pointed where he had been looking and gave the binoculars to Euan. Euan looked hard for a moment and then asked Mark to check the distant ship's direction and speed through the radar on the starboard side of the wheel house.

Mark looked into the radar monitor and said "Yes, that must be her. She's doing about 16 to 18 knots. She will pass us about a mile or more off our portside on her present course."

Ellis said to Euan. "Do you know if the Captain or Malloss have a repeater compass below? We need to alter course gently a point or two to port, without alerting either the Captain or Malloss. We also do not want to give the ferry the impression we are going to turn across her bows, as she may blow the horn or radio us, yet it would help to be as near to her as possible."

"Yes, I can do that. It will eventually become clear to the Captain at least, as I think there is a repeater in the saloon, and he will come to see what I am doing, but we should get away with it for several minutes with any luck."

"Do it," said Ellis. "We need to attract her attention. Mark, I assume there are distress flares somewhere up here?"

"Yes, that locker on the starboard side. There is a good stock, including red and white rocket flares, a reasonable number of hand held ones and several smoke floats."

"Right. This is what I suggest."

He explained what he had in mind, ending "Hal, you have one arm out of use, so I suggest Euan hands the wheel to you, so he can help with the plan and if a fight develops as I'm afraid it will. Malloss' goons will be spoiling for it. They will think they have something to loose. I wonder how Simon will react. He did not join in when Hal was stabbed did he? We will probably have to cope with Grumpy and the captain too.

Mark, give us two or three hand flares and a couple of rocket flares each. You two will know how to use them but neither Vaila nor I are familiar with them so can you ensure we understand how to set them off?"

Mark said, "There are instructions written on them. The basic thing is that you pull the loop at the bottom of the holder, whichever flare or float you have, gripping the holder firmly. Point it away from you, we do not want to set fire to ourselves – especially with the rocket flares."

Ellis suggested that Vaila had the smoke floats and sat between himself and the stern. "I also suggest you give Vaila most of the rest to hide behind her back out of sight if- or more likely when - any crew appear." Mark immediately came over to Ellis and Vaila and explained how to use the flares and floats. He told Vaila that the smoke floats should be set off and immediately thrown over the side into the sea.

"They will," he said, "burn for several minutes, unlike the hand held flares that last only a minute or so each. If you think it would help, you could throw one forward over the wheel house, it will make a fog all round us if needed."

Ellis said "I hope we will be able to hold our fire, so to speak, until the ferry is quite near us, but if anyone has noticed our course change before that we will have to act at once, and certainly before Grumpy, Sid and Bill can get here. Ideally, we would start with the rocket flares – we have at least two each – and fire them at minute intervals, one at a time, but if Sid and co. get here just keep them going for as long as you can. You can fire the smoke floats at the same time Vaila, just keep firing them whilst we keep the goons at bay. All of us can also use the hand held-flares. Just remember they are fireworks. Hold them away from you."

"Hal, as soon as we are discovered and start to fire the rocket flares push the engine to maximum speed and head for the ferry directly."

"Mark, Malloss must have a radio? Is there any way to disable it?"

"Only by turning off all the electrics from here – he pointed to the switch on the panel in front of Euan. But it would only take a minute to turn the radio over to emergency batteries at the radio itself. But why does it matter?"

"Because Malloss may radio the ferry to try to suggest we are OK. If, for any reason, the ferry does not stop we have had it; we are outnumbered."

"Anyone any other ideas? Otherwise that's all we can do. Just pray that the plan works."

He looked to see where the ferry was. He reckoned it was still six to seven miles away, possibly more. He smiled at Vaila to encourage her, but thought she looked determined enough; she said nothing just smiled back.

Ellis thought the ferry was around five miles away when the double doors of the hatch were thrown open by the Captain. They all looked as innocent as they could, but of course with Hal in the helmsman's seat and Euan and Mark either side of him the Captain realized at once things were not as he had ordered.

"Why are we on this course? What in heavens name are you doing letting one of the prisoners touch the wheel?" He did not wait for an answer before yelling through the open hatch, "Simon, why the hell are you not up here helping with the prisoners?" At the same moment Ellis pulled out his hand holding a rocket flare from behind Vaila, and pulled the loop on the base of the holder and the rocket shot into the air, bursting high above them.

The Captain grabbed the phone by Hal simultaneously pressing one of the buttons. It was answered at once and he shouted, "Sid, all of you. Up to the cockpit - now". Mark immediately fired the second rocket. The Captain was about to shout through the hatch again when he was stopped by

Mark who put his hand over the Captains mouth to keep him quiet and threw him to the deck.

A moment or so later, Simon came through the hatch. He stood there, half in and half out, uncertain what to do.

Vaila pulled the ring on a smoke float and threw it over the side. Without waiting to see the result she pulled the ring on the second one and hurled over the roof of the wheel house to land on the deck, where it started to pour out thick white smoke, just before Sid and Bill, who had appeared through the fore hatch, started to run down the side deck towards them followed by Grumpy. The smoke quickly enveloped them – hiding them from the cockpit and the view of anything forward of the wheel house.

Euan just had time to fire the third rocket before they arrived through the smoke. Sid knocked him to the deck. He landed on the Captain just as he was trying to get up.

Simon, seeing what Vaila was doing, ran the two or three steps to her shouting, "Stop that."

As he did so she reached behind her back, grabbed a flare in her right hand and put her first finger of her left hand through the loop and pointed it at Simon

"No, get off me."

"Come on. You can't win. You'll get hurt. Come with me." He reached for the hand held out towards him holding the flare pointed at him. He gripped her wrist hard. "Come on."

"I'd prefer to die first, let go!"

But Simon tightened his hold on her wrist. "Then die you bitch."

He pulled her up as hard as he could by her right hand, attempting to pull her to the rail, clearly meaning to throw her overboard. But in doing so he effectively pulled the loop from the flare she was holding. It fired just as Vaila was forced to let go of it by his tightening fingers. It fell to the deck partly on his shoe, the flame on his trouser bottom and sock. It set them alight instantly, he screamed, let go of her and tried to put the flame out, but could not do so. He did the only thing he could think of, jumped up on the seat and over the side to quench the flames.

Bill rushed at Ellis as Sid moved towards Mark. Bill hit Ellis hard in the face and he staggered back to land on the seat where Vaila had been – she was now standing holding the rail and looking over the side. Although hurt he jumped straight up at Bill who stepped back, and tripped over the Captain still on the deck, as he was starting to get up. The Captain fell back a second time and Bill fell backwards over him onto the deck. Sid attempted to hit Mark, but missed. He was off balance as Mark pushed him against the edge of the wheel house so hard that it knocked the breath out of him. It only stopped him for a moment. As Bill got up Grumpy joined in as Ellis stepped forward to tackle Bill again, but Ellis was distracted by Simon's attack on Vaila, and failed to avoid Grumpy's kick, which caught him hard on the ankle. Grumpy then pushed Ellis back whilst he was off balance. He staggered back to discover how painful his ankle was, and again fell onto the seat by Vaila.

Ellis saw that Sid had his knife in his hand, threatening Mark who was nearest him. A couple of times Mark dodged the knife but then Sid's knife cut a long gash across his chest. Ellis seeing Mark in trouble, reached into the little store of flares that had been behind Vaila, picked up the first flare that his fingers found, pointed it at Sid and pulled the loop. Only then did he realize that it was a white rocket flare. The rocket fired and hit Sid on the arm that held the knife, which he dropped. The rocket was deflected to streak straight through the hatch that Simon had left open, into the saloon. He heard a scream, and saw Andy flee through the far door as the white phosphorous star shell burst. In the confined space the whole saloon seemed to be engulfed in a brilliant white flame, and worse, the rocket had hit a decorative paraffin lamp on the wall. The lamp was broken and fell out of its gimbal onto the deck spilling paraffin that the shell immediately set alight.

This distraction and the pain to his arm caused Sid to pause. Euan kept his cool. He bent down, picked up Sid's knife and threw it overboard. But Sid did not stop to watch it, he hit Euan as he stood up. He fell, and in a momentary flash of comedy landed on the Captain, as he tried to get up for the third time.

Bill decided to leave Ellis, and go for Hal who had the engine at full throttle. Hal dodged his punch but inadvertently spun the wheel as he did so. He lost his balance and fell to the deck, no longer in control of Gaia Marina. The movement of the yacht, as it healed into a sharp turn at full speed, caught Bill off balance for a moment, during which he noticed Ellis, beside Vaila recovering from Grumpy's attentions. Grumpy looked at Bill nodding his head towards Ellis indicating that they should now attack him.

Ellis, seeing this, realized they were now in a losing position. Hal, and Mark, were unable to do much more, Vaila, beside him seemed stunned, repeating almost to herself, "I didn't mean to kill him."

Ellis thought she was in shock, and doubted if she could help either. Only Euan and himself would be able to resist, and perhaps not for long.

Of their assailants Sid looked stunned by the rocket, or the loss of his favourite knife, or both. The Captain was still on the deck apparently hesitant about trying to get up again. He would recover soon enough. Bill and Grumpy were unhurt and briefly spoke to each other again looking at Ellis. It was easy to guess what they were thinking. Grumpy shouted at Sid and Bill "Come on, what are you bloody well waiting for?" as he and Bill moved forward.

"Stop all that." Malloss' voice cut through the chaos in a bellow and in the sudden brief silence the sound, as well as the sight of fire, brought them all to see the common danger.

Malloss shouted "The yacht is on fire. Stop this brawl and put the fire out." He had come via the fore hatch and the deck, being unable to get through the saloon. This had meant he had come through the smoke. None of them had seen him coming.

For once Sid and Bill looked less aggressive and Grumpy seemed confused and unsure what to do. They recognized that Malloss was right. "We'll get you later." Sid said to Ellis as he turned to Malloss for instructions, ignoring Grumpy. For next few minutes Sid, Bill and Grumpy followed the directions Malloss gave them. Malloss himself turned off the engine, to prevent the wind fanning the flames, so that the yacht gradually came to a stop. Luckily the sea was calm.

Realising that they were being temporarily ignored, Ellis quickly whispered to Vaila, "Go into the stern cabin, if you think it will take us all. I'll tell the others. We might be able to hold out there for a bit." It was, of course a desperate plan and as he said it he could not help a fleeting thought 'hold out for what?' In any event Vaila seemed unable to take in what he had said. She just looked over the side of the yacht and said "Where is he? Did I kill him? I didn't want him to die, Oh Lord help me, am I a murderer?"

"No darling you are a very brave girl who had to defend herself."

She did not seem to accept his words, perhaps even hear them. She looked inconsolable. Worse, she was clearly so stunned by what had happened that she seemed rooted to the spot. Ellis felt completely defeated. He thought his plan had failed in spite of all they had done. Once the fire was out then what would happen? Was he, or any of them, going to be able to do anything now?

But they had all forgotten about the ferry, partly because the smoke float Vaila had thrown onto the deck had only just stopped spewing out thick white smoke and partly as *Gaia Marina* had gone round in circles when Hal had lost control, which had been disorienting for them all.

It had not been long since Ellis had fired the first distress rocket, but in that time the Ferry had reached them and was now only 50 yards away, stopped. Hal, Euan and Mark had joined Ellis and Vaila at the rear of the cockpit when two of the ferry's boats came across to *Gaia Marina*.

Malloss, Grumpy, the Captain, Sid and Bill were so preoccupied trying to put the fire out that they were taken by surprise at the arrival of the boats. They soon appreciated the extra hands and firefighting equipment, with which, added to the yacht's own extinguishers, the fire was brought under control.

Whilst the rest were fighting the fire, Ellis introduced himself to the ferry's officer in charge of the boats crew. He said "Thank goodness you are here. Please could you take the girl to the ferry with those injured, she seems to be in shock. I am worried about her. I'll see what I can do here. But tell your boat crews that those two are dangerous," indicating Sid and Bill. "I would be glad to have help here to keep the peace, if you could spare someone."

"Don't worry, we were radioed about this yacht, we know the situation. My orders are to take charge until the police boat gets here. The Captain said to bring everyone on the yacht to the ferry, the yacht's crew in one boat and your party in the other, including the wounded."

"Thank you and thank goodness you got here in time. But two of the yacht's crew were with us, Euan and Mark. They should be with us in our boat." Ellis introduced Euan and Mark to make sure no mistake was made. Malloss had soon realized that Euan and Mark had been helping Hal and Ellis, and had already sworn at them as traitors.

"Very well"

Malloss now saw Ellis talking to the officer at the back of the cockpit and came across. Indicating Ellis he said to the officer "I want that man arrested and held particularly closely. He is responsible for this. Put him in one of your boats and get him to the ferry at once. The other can take my men and myself. Then I must be returned to the mainland with all speed. The rest of Mackenzie's party must stay here until that is done."

"My orders are to take you and your crew in one boat and Mr MacKenzie and all his party in the other to the ferry. I have no authority to arrest anyone, and certainly not Mr MacKenzie."

"I am giving the orders to arrest MacKenzie. On my yacht you will obey my orders. That is sufficient authority."

"I am responsible to my Captain, Sir. I would be obliged if you could cooperate."

"I shall speak to your Captain about your refusal to do as I have asked."

"Very well Sir, but in the meantime please will you get into the boat."

"I assume you will ensure the safety of this Yacht. She is to be taken straight to a mainland port that can carry out repairs. Detail some of your more competent men to do so."

"A police launch is on its way, as is the lifeboat. They will decide where the yacht is taken, probably the nearest port, St Margaret's Hope, where you can make whatever arrangements you wish."

"Are you again refusing my orders? Do you know who I am?"

"I regret Sir that I can only take orders from my Captain. Now I must ask you to get into the boat for transfer to the ferry."

Ellis heard one of the boats crew say very quietly "Poor fellow, not knowing his own name." It was an old joke but it did Ellis a lot of good to hear it.

The yacht's crew, including Malloss who, however angry, could only do as he was asked, got into the first boat. As he sat down he glared at Ellis, still on the yacht. Ellis could not hear what he said but obviously it was not complimentary.

Once the first boat had gone, Vaila, Hal, Euan and Mark got into the second boat with Ellis' help for Hal and Mark, though his own ankle was now swelling up. It was painful but he was relieved to find no difficulty walking on it. As Ellis followed them into the boat Vaila suddenly turned to the Officer and said,

"One of the crew was burnt when his clothes were on fire, and jumped overboard to put the fire out. Have you seen him?"

"No, but if we circle the yacht before going to the ferry, we may spot him."

At that moment his radio beeped. He listened to the message and said "Yes Sir, we are on our way and have everyone except one, so I'm told. He went overboard. We will have a look before returning."

He listened to the response. "Thank you, Sir. Out" Turning to Vaila, he said "That was the ferry Captain. He told me that there is debris in the water beyond the yacht. We'll go round and see what it is."

"Thank you."

As they circled Gaia Marina, one of the crew pointing, shouted "There, is that him?"

Simon was alive when they picked him up, but clearly in a bad way. He was hardly conscious. Vaila sat and watched him until they were taken on board the ferry and he was taken below for treatment, along with Hal and Mark. Euan went with them.

163

Ellis and Vaila were given a cabin, and a cup of hot strong coffee. Ellis asked if he could see his friends, but the Captain, who had just come into the cabin, said it was better to leave the staff to do what they could first. "Give them ten minutes." At least, Ellis thought, Vaila, although very quiet, seemed better. She sat next to him, leaning on him.

The Captain said to Vaila, "I presume as the only lady involved you must be Vaila Flett?" She nodded "And are you Ellis MacKenzie?" to which Ellis agreed.

"Well," said the Captain, "First can I introduce myself, I am Captain Mike Jamieson. You are clearly the heroes today. We had a call from Mr Wilson telling us about your message to him. He has organised all sorts of support. He will be at St Margaret's Hope when we dock. He said to tell you that Triscoll of the Flotta terminal thinks you deserve a medal. They found and defused the bomb. He is longing to speak to you, something about the bomb being quite small and apparently pointless. He hopes you know more of why it was planted."

"I had wondered about that," Ellis said, "But my brain is in a whirl at the moment. If there is time before we get to St Margaret's, I would still like to see my friends before we get there – especially Hal Flett; he is Vaila's brother and she is anxious to see he is OK."

The Captain, using his radio, spoke to the sick bay, listened for a short while and said to Vaila and Ellis, "Your brother has only bruises to add to his injured arm, it is very uncomfortable but he should recover fully in time. Mark's cut, although dramatic, is superficial. One of the crew – Sid I think he is – has a burned arm – nothing serious, although he made a big fuss about it when he was treated. But the man picked up from the water is causing them concern. He has a substantial burn to his left leg, and must have come close to drowning. Having been in the water he has also suffered hypothermia. An ambulance has been arranged for him to go to the hospital as soon as we dock. I expect it will take the other wounded too.

You should also know that the police launch is accompanying us, and the life boat has the yacht in tow. There will be quite a police presence at the dock; the whole of the little Orkney force I'd think. The yacht's crew are subdued but you never know. Sir Frank is the only one of them to have made a scene, raging about the damage to his yacht, and has put the blame on you, Mr MacKenzie. I gather he had demanded your arrest even whilst still on the yacht. He was most unpleasant to my officer, who rightly told him to speak to me. Now he wants my officer disciplined as well as your arrest. He nearly exploded when I told him that all the yachts compliment, so the police tell me, will be under arrest for holding you and your friends against your will.

He threatens lawyers and goodness knows what else. So there will be an enquiry. Mr Wilson said to say that he would arrange everything for you once he had all the details.

Now I must return to the bridge as we are near St Margaret's. The steward will take you down to see your friends. I suggest you stay there, until we have disembarked the yacht's crew – we don't want any form of confrontation should they see you."

The small sick bay was full, with four of them in it, and felt crowded. The attendant, who introduced himself as Martin, was a steward with full first aid training. He had made Hal and Mark as comfortable as he could and Euan was helping, although his bruises were extremely uncomfortable. Euan was also keeping an eye on Sid, but after his treatment he had fallen asleep. Hal, Mark and Euan greeted Vaila and Ellis with enthusiasm, and assured them that their injuries would soon heal. Hal added that he would expect the best of nursing at the hospital, "After all I have my own private nurse" – a joke he had to explain to the others.

Ellis saw Vaila looking round; "Where is Simon?"

"Simon? The other man? I put him in the next room." Replied the steward, "He is in a far worse state than these two. You can visit him, but although I have done what I can for his burns, and tried to clear his lungs as well as keep him as warm as I can, I am unhappy with his condition. I think he should see a doctor as soon as possible. He keeps mumbling. It's hard to know what he is saying. I think he is delirious. He does not react when I speak to him."

Ellis and Vaila went into his cabin. Simon did not appear to recognize them. His mumbling seemed as if he spoke unaware of what he said himself, so Ellis guided Vaila out of the room. She said nothing, but he could see that she was shaken by the visit. They returned to the sick bay to stay with the others. Sid had by now been taken ashore, so they sat on his bunk.

Ellis said to Euan and Mark, "In case we do not get another chance, thank you so much for all you did for us in that fight. I am afraid though, you have lost your jobs with Malloss."

"Good riddance. Don't worry about us. I was already wondering if one of the ferry companies needed extra hands, and if not there is always the rigs." Said Euan.

Mark said cheerfully, as if his wound was nothing to him. "An honourable scar will be a reminder of a good rumble. I think I will enjoy telling my grandchildren – and the story will certainly get better the more often I tell it!"

One of the stewards came to the cabin after 20 minutes or so and said they could now disembark. He added, "Which of you is Mr MacKenzie?"

Ellis said "I am."

"As the yacht's crew were going down the gangplank, one of them, who had held back to be the last, thrust this into my hand. He said to give it to you. He pleaded with me to do so personally and begged me not to give away to the rest of the crew that he had given me anything. He seemed very scared of them.

The steward gave Ellis an envelope. Ellis saw his name written in pencil on it and he put it in his pocket.

The Aftermath

Ellis and Vaila were met as soon as they were ashore by Uncle John. He was clearly anxious about them, but once reassured he told them that the police were keen to take their statement as soon as possible.

As they watched Simon, Hal and Mark taken into the waiting ambulance, Ellis said, "Yes of course. But I am also a bit hungry; we had an early breakfast and no lunch, can we get something to eat and another hot drink to go with the statement?"

He was delighted when Vaila, sounding much more cheerful, teased him "Typical man, always hungry! But I suppose I should have something too. I am so relieved that Hal is now in good hands; I expect he will enjoy the nursing!

"Yes, Uncle John, we should get the statement over with as soon as possible. Mum & Dad must have heard something about all this and may be worried. Can we just ring them first?"

"I can do better than that. I will take you home. I have told them what was happening, and I have arranged that Detective Inspector Simmonds comes there to take your statement; you have had a bad time, so the Captain Jamieson tells me, so that is where you should be."

Ingrid and Ronald were delighted to see Vaila and Ellis back safely, even if Ellis' black eye was getting blacker. They made a comforting fuss of them and they soon had a light, and very late, meal on the kitchen table. Ingrid especially wanted to hear all about it. She was naturally also concerned about Hal, but Vaila reassured her that Hal was enjoying having Inga to look after him.

"We have a little time before Simmons arrives, so, although you will have to tell your story again to Simmonds would you mind telling us in as much detail as you can about what happened, while you eat?" Asked Uncle John.

Ellis, said to Ingrid, "I am afraid you may be horrified with the threats made against Vaila, but it would perhaps help us both to tell you about it."

With some help from Vaila Ellis explained what had happened. He ended by saying how much they appreciated Uncle John's help by alerting the authorities to their predicament.

"It was lucky that I got the text – I do not always check it. I have the feeling you would have escaped anyway, but I am just glad I could make it rather easier for you."

Ingrid said "Vaila, I am so sorry you had to go through all that. I hope Malloss and the others get the punishment they deserve. Nor do I wish to ever hear from Smith again."

They had hardly finished both the meal and the story when the bell rang. It was Detective Inspector Simmons.

Ingrid made coffee for them, while Ellis and Vaila repeated their account of the day's events for Detective Inspector Simmons. Once he had heard the story, his questions were mainly about detail and about those involved in the story. He ended by saying that Malloss and all of the yachts crew except Euan, Mark and Andy were facing a variety of charges, although they were leaving any charges against Simon until he was well enough to be properly interviewed. Although Andy Hitchens, was currently held

169

with the rest of the crew, he would be released in the morning as he had played no part in the action on either Flotta or on Gaia Marina. Euan and Mark had not been arrested and their help to Ellis, Hal and Vaila was recognized. He added "It is now approaching 6pm so I think those arrested will all stay under lock and key for tonight, but doubtless will be given bail tomorrow morning. No doubt Sir Frank will be furious at being held even for one night, so I suppose we will have to ensure he is comfortable enough to think he is being treated as a knight should be or we will never hear the last of it."

Uncle John asked, "Do you think there will be any bail conditions?"

As all but one of the yachts crew are not Orcadians, I suppose they may be told to remain in Orkney, or maybe – if they want to leave – to notify the police of where they will be."

After D I Simmons had left Ellis had a grin on his face.

"What are you looking so happy about Ellis?"

"I assume the initial cases will be heard here in Orkney over the next few weeks?" When Uncle John nodded assent he said "Then for me there is a silver lining. Not only will I have a good excuse for coming to Orkney, but if they pay expenses I'll even get some free rides!"

"I'd wish for a better reason, but I think I know the attraction!" Replied Uncle John with a smile. Vaila wondered why she only seemed to blush in front of Uncle John, although it was even worse to blush in front of her Mum and Dad, but she said nothing, hoping they had not noticed.

Ronald added "You know, John, I think it would be as well that Ellis returns as much as possible, otherwise with Hal out of action who is going to get Vaila out of the scrapes she gets herself into!" Ellis noticed the mischievous grin on his face. Vaila looked embarrassed.

Simon

Hal did not need to stay overnight in the hospital after his arm had been stitched. But the wound had to be dressed each day. He had persuaded the doctor that the dressing should be done by his own favourite nurse rather than the district nurse. So the next morning Inga came shortly after breakfast. She told Vaila and Ellis that she had something important to discuss with them. She suggested the four of them had a coffee together after the wound had been dressed.

Inga's news concerned Simon. "Simon has been asking to see you, Vaila. He seems desperate that you should visit him because, he said, he has something he needs to ask you. He told me to say that you should come with Ellis, and promises that what he wants to say will not upset you. He seems quite worried about something, and generally very distressed. He has not told me what it is, and I felt it might be best not to press him on it.

"I have talked to the doctor and a psychologist who is seeing him, and explained that you would probably be very reluctant to come, but the psychologist said that if you could see Simon, it might help him. Apparently there is concern that his mental state is impeding his recovery from the burns and the damage to his lungs. It's up to you, Vaila, no one could blame you for refusing. But would you consider it?"

Ellis was surprised at first by Vaila's immediate reply, "Of course I'll come, it might be good for me too. Can we come at once so I do not have time to think about it too much? I do want Ellis to be with me." She sounded nervous but determined.

They borrowed Hal's car and when they arrived at the hospital, Inga's presence ensured they went into the single room Simon was in at once.

He lay in the bed unmoving, and looked dopy from the medication, but he was awake and said, "Thank you so much for coming. Please…. sit down." He paused "Sorry, I find it hard to concentrate. I….I want so much to ask for your forgiveness Vaila." His hesitant speech gave evidence of his mental confusion.

"Vaila, I want to say how sorry I am for….for all I have said and done to you. I ….I wanted to apologize as deeply as I can. I suppose…. my feelings for you got out of control. I had ….never met anyone like you. You were always so kind and…. straight with me but I failed to understand…. How you thought of me I mean…. What you felt. What you expected of me…. I thought…. only of what I wanted….. it never occurred to me you were different. Different, kindness. Friendship, not…you know. When Ellis came along I was jealous. …..I think I knew from the start he was a better man than me….you said he was just…. a work colleague, but….. I could see how much you liked him. I saw you together…you and him together several times, and I could see …..you were growing closer to each other…..I knew I was making a fool of myself trying to persuade you return to me…..what else could I do?……in my heart I knew I had lost…. I could not admit it, or accept it even to myself …. My….my jealousy drove me insane. I couldn't stop thinking about you… I could not stop imagining you in his arms.... It haunted me day and night.... I could not let go. I wanted.... revenge then because you preferred him to me. If you were not to be mine.... nor should you be his .... I was so horrible to you in my jealousy. It took me over......On the ....on the yacht... in desperation I thought if I forced you to marry me you would come to love me...but ....In the fight you said you'd die before coming with me. I went mad and tried to kill you...

After the boat from the ferry picked me up, I heard the crew talking..... One of them said 'Thank goodness the girl insisted on our searching. We would never have found him otherwise.' It could only have been.... you... I was astonished, amazed...I could hardly believe it ...... you actually asked them to look for me and rescue me..... Even though only just....just before, I had made such terrible threats.... Had even tried to throw you overboard..... You actually wanted me to be rescued....It haunted me...... Anyone else would have been happy if I drowned..... Others...wouldn't have given me a second thought after all I had done. It....it brought me to my senses." He paused a long minute then continued.

"All I can think of now is how horrible I have been to you. I have become stupid....Horrid...hateful. Perhaps if ......if you forgave me..... I do not deserve it, but ....but I so want you to. Would you? You did like me once, before I went wrong ....Didn't you?... Please? I promise I will never trouble you again.... whatever you do or say, but if.....but if I felt you had forgiven me....maybe I would feel free of what I did. Maybe after I get prison.. ...I deserve ...it... for attempting to hurt you...to throw into the sea..... ...I will move south.....start again. I don't want to be like that...again..ever But how can...I mean maybe ...How I can start again with all the..... dreadful things I did...still in my head? Free of them.... being forgiven maybe I could do things better, help people, not use them for my own amusement.... Please, please, Vaila?" He pleaded. He looked as if he meant it. He had tears on his cheek.

She replied "I was worried I had killed you with that flare, so I am glad you are recovering and ..."

Simon interrupted, this time much less hesitantly "No you didn't, it was my fault. I grabbed your hand so that you were bound to drop the flare, so it was all my own fault. I deserved to die. In the water, knowing I had lost you I thought of just going under.....It was terrible, and the nightmare keeps returning. If only I had not been so stupid, selfish, cruel, thoughtless." His voice faded away and there was another silence.

Then Vaila stood up, looking down at him lying in the hospital bed, she appeared resolute, compassionate and very sad. She said "Yes Simon, I will forgive you and all you did and said to me. In spite of everything I would like you to remember me with affection, not in your nightmares. But it is best that we do not meet again for both of us. Now we must go."

She bent down and kissed him briefly, turned away, and left the room.

As Ellis stood up to follow her, Simon said "Ellis, look after her. She is very special and I so wish I had seen it from the start. Maybe you'll marry her - that would be good."

Ellis could hardly hear his words, so quietly spoken were they, but he understood. "I will do my best for her, you can be sure of that. Good bye and good luck Simon."

There was a long silence when they returned to the car. Ellis took his time starting it, and then said "What would you like to do now?"

Vaila said "Please just drive somewhere. If I just sit here I will burst into tears."

As he drove, Ellis remained silent. He was not sure whether to leave her to her thoughts or whether he should say something, and eventually said "Vaila, that was a truly Christian thing you did for Simon, and I think he appreciated it. I believe he will do as he said; he will go elsewhere and try to start again. He is, I suspect and hope, a changed man, and the credit for that is entirely yours. It must have cost you a great deal of anguish.

"Now it is my job to help you to recover. We will stop somewhere for a coffee and an indulgent piece of sticky cake. We will talk about pleasant things. After that I should tell Uncle John about Simon. He may also be able to tell us how the bail hearings went."

She smiled at him, but only a few moments later his mobile rang. He gave it to Vaila to answer.

"Hello, Ellis MacKenzie's phone. He is driving just now." ....

"Oh how good to hear from you. We have just been to the hospital and saw Mark; he is as cheerful as ever, teasing Inga by telling her a whole load of rubbish about what Hal had got up to! How are you? What can we do for you?"

She listened for a full minute, "Where is he now?"

.... "OK. Poor Andy. We'll come at once; I think I know who can help him. See you shortly. Good bye."

She turned to Ellis, "That was Euan. He is with Andy who he met wandering down the street in a very unhappy and worried frame of mind. I said we'd come and see what we could do to help."

"Where are they?"

"They are at a cafe called The Coffee Pot. I think I mentioned it to you once? It's by the Cathedral. You can get me a coffee there. I'll direct you."

ANDY

They arrived at the Coffee Pot and found Euan with Andy who was indeed looking very distressed. When they had ordered, Ellis asked Andy what the problem was.

He replied, "They let me out this morning; I am not to be charged with anything, the detective man recommended I was released. On my way out of the place, I had to pass Malloss, and he said, 'Remember you must keep quiet for Ada's sake. If you tell anyone about either the bank or anything that happened on the yacht, I will find out.' But I already had told you everything in my letter – did you get it?"

"Yes I did, and we understand, Andy. Only one other person has seen the letter and he is the man who can help you. We will take you somewhere safe until Malloss goes. We must find a way to get Ada and yourself together, perhaps here in Orkney."

"Yes, but please, Malloss must not know I am with you. He is a horrid man. I am so frightened that he will hurt her.

176

He said he would move her somewhere so that I would never see her again, as soon as he got home to Edinburgh if I said another word."

He looked as if he was so worried for Ada that he was near to tears, and Ellis could not help thinking that his concern was all too justified.

"Vaila can you fetch Hals car, I am sure he would not mind if we use it again while mine is still at the Houton ferry pier – was it really only yesterday we left it there?"

While Vaila was fetching the car, Ellis rang Uncle John. He said

"We have seen Simon and should tell you what happened. We have also met Andy, Malloss' sort of servant, who wrote the letter I gave you. He has been released but has nowhere to go. Can I bring him to Stromness?"

"That is an excellent idea. There is a small flat above the office here that Andy could use, and we need to talk to him about the letter."

"Very well. Vaila is just fetching Hal's car and we will pick mine up at Houton on our way. See you as soon as we can do that." He said nothing of Andy's state of mind, or his fear of Malloss and his threats. He did not wish to do so in front of Andy.

Uncle John saw them in his Stromness office. He asked how Vaila and Ellis felt after a night's rest, and they reassured him they were more or less recovered. He then spoke kindly to Andy. "I am so sorry you have had to go through such unhappy times with Malloss. Let's see what we can do to help both your wife and yourself."

They installed Andy in the flat above the office. He had nothing beyond the clothes he was wearing, his few possessions still being on Gaia Marina. Uncle John told him to go to the gentleman's tailor shop across the street and buy what he needed telling him to put it on his account. Andy was overwhelmed by this generosity, and Uncle John had to reassure him that he really meant it.

"We must have you looking like an Orcadian." He said with a smile, and Andy was persuaded to do as Uncle John suggested.

As soon as Andy had left, Ellis told Uncle John that he had taken Vaila to the hospital to visit Simon at his request, and what had happened. "Simon ended by saying he will move away, and try to start again. After Vaila had left the room he actually asked me to look after Vaila and even said - oh never mind."

"You always amaze me Vaila," said Uncle John. It really was an extremely kind and wonderful thing to do." Vaila said nothing, she looked a bit embarrassed.

He continued "We must now consider what else we need to do. In real life you cannot end your story with a dramatic escape. Like a good meal there is always the washing up, and in this case the pots are so dirty that there are still some difficult things to deal with.

I do not want you worried, but nor should you take it all too lightly, so I will just say that Malloss and his friends are bound to mount a vigorous defense to the criminal charges. After all the charges are serious and there are several of them, including the bomb, assault, and holding you without your consent, plus threats of forced marriage, rape and murder. They may suggest you were to blame, at least in part, or might be to try to blacken your name. All absurd in your eyes of course, and uncomfortable, but it only demands you keep calm and tell the truth as you see it. I will be there to support you. Otherwise so much for the criminal case, at this stage anyway.

Next there is Andy's letter. Clearly the police and prosecution should have it, but the moment they read it they are bound to take action which will, in turn, make it clear to Malloss that Andy has told us his story.   You have both read it?"

Vaila said "No I have not seen it, and Ellis only read it briefly."

"Then you should. Jean has made a typewritten version. Here is a copy – I suggest you read it now but do not take it out of the office; the original and these transcriptions should remain in my safe until given to the police. I cannot hold it here for long; I am stretching my reputation by holding it back at all. As you read it, bear in mind that it is not only important to the criminal case against Malloss but also significant for you too because Malloss wants to sue you for the damage to the yacht."

Transcript of a note addressed to Mr. Ellis MacKenzie.

N.B. The hand written pencil note has neither date nor address. It was delivered by hand via a steward on the Pentland ferry. In transcribing it I have corrected the English.

Jean Davidson, P.A. to John Wilson, Solicitor, Stromness.

Dear Mr. MacKenzie,

Please Sir, can you help me, I don't know what to do. You seem a kind man and I am desperate to escape Malloss. This is what happened to Ada and me. If you can't help me we have had it. Malloss will kill me if he knows I have written this, or worse, take it out on Ada. I must try to get it to you secretly.

My name is Andy Hitchens, I am 33 years of age, and have been stuck on the yacht for about 6 months. This is what happened to me and my Ada. I swear on the Bible it is the truth, so far as I know and remember it.

About 3 years ago I was employed by the Great Northern Bank in Edinburgh as the junior assistant in the post and administration dept.

My job was to take files, statements, stationery etc. to the offices as instructed. I also did photo copying and filing. I sometimes took the mail to the post office. I was told I was reliable and worked hard, and I was increasingly given messages to deliver around Edinburgh, for example some large parcels to be given to an office, or sometimes to someone personally.

I liked these jobs I not only felt good delivering important stuff but it was more fun than being in the office all day.

In that big office I was nothing. The secretaries worked in a large room. I suppose they were good at their jobs, but they gossiped all the time. Some of them were very pretty and I especially fancied one, called Fiona. I thought she was beautiful. I worshipped her, but of course I hardly even spoke to her, and she hardly seemed to see me. One day I decided to risk asking her out. I thought she could only say no. Of course I should have known. When I asked her, she just laughed at me. "Why on earth would I want to go out with you? I have invitations from men from the best families in Scotland."

The snub would have been OK except that she told all the other secretaries; they thought it funny and after that I could hardly go near the typing pool without some of them teasing me – "Here's Fiona's true love." Or "What has Fiona got that I haven't?" Even, when she was nearby, "Fiona, here's your frustrated boyfriend. Don't you love him anymore?" And they would all jeer and laugh at me. I hated it.

I kept working at the bank because of the errands around the town. The more senior staff gave me more and more jobs like that. They began to trust me. I was able to get back at the secretaries who teased me by refusing to carry their messages. I would say 'The Chief Financial Officer has work for me, or 'I have no time for mere secretaries as I am working for the directors.' They may not have believed me but they got tired of being nasty to me.

Then I met Ada. She was the tea lady. Well I knew her anyway, I mean I actually got to talk to her. She did not like going to the typing pool also, a load of catty snobs she called them. She had a little kitchen, and I started helping her wash up and put everything away before going home. She is the same age as me. Ada is kind and homely. We became good friends at work, then we went out together most weekends, and then more like lovers when we could although we kept it secret from our parents.

We both lived with our parents in their council houses. But we could not get married because neither parents would

181

allow us to stay with them together even if we were married. We looked for a house, but could not afford the rent on any we saw, and to buy was impossible. We could not even get a council house. Getting married was just a dream.

One day I was called into Sir Frank Malloss office. He was of course the Chief Executive, it said so on the door. I had never been there before, I never had expected to see it. It was very posh, full of antiques and had a beautiful carpet. The view out of the large window was over to Arthur's Seat.

He told me that a number of his colleagues had told him that I could be trusted with highly confidential documents. He gave me a green document, with lots of figures and things.

I was asked to photo copy it three times, to do so onto green copy paper and to do the job after everyone had gone home. No one must see what I was doing. Lastly he said that he presumed I could be trusted not to read it myself. He said that I would be unlikely to understand it anyway.

When I had copied it I was to put each copy, and the original, into plain, unaddressed envelopes. Deliver them to him personally at home that evening he said. I was told he would make it worth my while. I did it the way he said.

After that there were several other occasions I was given similar jobs to do and each time I would get a bonus in my pay packet. Other senior staff also started to give me personal jobs. I even had to deliver stuff to a girl who was obviously one of the director's girlfriend's, and I knew he was married. That shows how much I was trusted, I thought at the time.

Sir Frank Malloss spoke to me about these extra jobs one evening when I delivered something to his house. He

182

told me how important it was that no one knew about the jobs I had done for him. If anyone ever asked me about them I was to say that I did them out of hours because they were urgent. I was to say that I did not read any of them and could say I did not understand what little I saw. I did not mind that, it would be no lie anyway.

He then asked me to do one very special errand. It was a simple thing, he said, a single copy to go to someone in London, at a café; he told me where it was. You must take it personally; go on the early train, deliver it and return on a train getting back no sooner than eight at night. I was to ring in before I left home to leave a message on the office answer phone that I was not feeling well and would have to take a day's sick leave. He stressed that no one must know I had even been to London. Nor was I told the name of the man I was to meet, I did not need to as he would recognize me. I must not claim anything on expenses from the bank. He gave me cash for the train and lunch etc., from his pocket and told me that by the end of the week I would have a very special bonus for doing this, which he promised, would solve our problem, Ada and me. I don't know how he knew about us. I did not think about that then.

It all seemed easy, and I quite enjoyed the trip. The only thing was that I did see someone else from the bank on the train going down – it was Fiona. She saw me, but she pretended she did not know me. I said nothing, I did not like her anymore.

The next day Sir Frank summoned me to his office. He asked how the trip went and I told him it was fine. I had delivered the document as he had asked me to do into the hand of the person he had told me to give it to. I did not mention seeing Fiona; I did not think it important, I wasn't sure that he would have known who she was anyway.

Not only that, but I couldn't think of anything except what he gave us - a little house. Ada and I were so happy. I realized there was a small mortgage to pay, I do not know about such things. All I knew was that we had the house, and could pay a little amount each month. We got married, just Ada and me. Even our Mums did not know, they thought we were living together not married and said they did not want to know what we did.

When the newspapers got stories about him and hinted that he was doing bad deals under the counter I did wonder if my secret trip to London was one of them. When some people were asking staff about what Sir Frank did, I said nothing. No one thinks a mere delivery person like me can do anything, no one sees us most of the time. We don't matter.

I expect you know about the things that led to Sir Frank being sacked better than me. I may have been trusted, but I was still only an errand boy. But I know he was sacked, he did not willingly resign, because I heard the row going on in his office with the big directors etc. and heard some of the talk about a deal to pay him off.

In the end we were all told that the bank was bust, and many would lose their jobs. There was to be an enquiry. Many staff were questioned and there was a lot of blame going around. The senior people were desperate to find a goat (or whatever it is when someone gets all the blame.) The heads of department were questioned, like my boss, and they looked at those below them to blame; they were all trying to save themselves by ratting on someone else.

I found myself in big trouble because of the house. How was I to know? They told me that Malloss had arranged a loan to me for the house from the bank and then somehow got the bank paying most of the interest etc. to itself but in my name. I don't know how it happened. First they wanted to know how a mere post boy should get such a big bonus, and then said that I must pay the proper interest on the mortgage. Of course I could not pay. I was in despair. Worse I was thought to have fiddled getting the bank to pay the interest.

I was asked why Malloss gave me the house. I said I ran errands for him but at first they said I was lying. I was to see someone very senior the next day.

That night Malloss rang me. He said he could fix everything, but there were three things I must do. I must never tell anyone about the London trip. I must say that I asked for a mortgage. And that I thought it was as it should be. You have a copy of the mortgage agreement that says the small amount I was paying, so show it to them, he said. It cannot be disputed he said. Just say you had asked Malloss if I could have a mortgage, that he had recommended me for one as a loyal servant of the bank, but that he had had nothing to do with the detail. He laughed about how the blame would fall on the mortgage department for their mistake, and as my document was legal it could not be changed.

I did as he asked. It worked out too, to start with. The new boss of the bank accepted the mortgage as genuine and said that in the circumstances the bank would accept the mortgage as genuine. It seemed as if all was going to be OK for us.

185

But then that girl Fiona – must have been her – ruined everything. How was I to know that her father was some important man in some company who was helping sort out the bank? She told her dad that she had seen me on the train to London. He seemed to know it was connected to some rotten deal Sir Frank had done. But they came heavy on me about my lie. I denied it. I said I was often asked to deliver stuff and I just did as I was told. I never looked at it. They went on and on about it. I had to tell them who I gave the London package to, they said. They didn't believe me when I said I did not know the name of the man I met at the café. In the end they had to give up, but they sacked me from the bank.

So we could not pay the mortgage payments, even the smaller ones with only Ada working on the minimum wage. I decided to tell Malloss; it was a terrible mistake. He said both Ada and I could work for him. You can keep the house, but Ada's job meant she must live in. We had a room in the top floor. She cleaned, & I did odd jobs etc. You could let the house, he said and then you can afford the mortgage. I believed him. It was OK at first. Then someone in the bank discovered about the letting, and said I had broken the terms of the mortgage – the only way the bank official told me – I could continue was if we paid the full mortgage interest, but the rent we got and the small wage Malloss paid, after deductions for our room and keep, was not enough. Malloss must have known that. He said to me that I was to give the bank a lump sum so the mortgage was only very small again – and he gave me cash to do it. Tell the bank you won a bit on the lottery.

At last we seemed to have everything OK. We had the house. We could afford the mortgage, and we had jobs that seemed OK.

Then he said he wanted me to come on the yacht to cook and clean. Just for a voyage, a couple of weeks. I wanted to stay with Ada but he insisted so he took me with him. Since then he has made me stay, I am never allowed on land. I hate it, I get sick. Some of the crew are OK, and I manage to keep out of the way of the latest ones. After a bit, a few weeks, I told him I wanted to see Ada, I wanted to go home. He got nasty. If I did not do exactly as I was told that he would tell the bank, and the police I stole the money from him to pay off part of the mortgage and then we would lose the house and I would go to prison. He told me to remember Ada was under Lady Malloss' control. Then letters from Ada stopped coming. I sent lots to her but no reply and I did not know what had happened. When I asked him how she was he told me she must be tired of writing, but I could not believe that. I was afraid she was ill or something.

I was cleaning his work cabin one day. By accident I pulled out a draw and saw all the letters I had sent to her, and some she had sent to me. He must have been preventing them being posted. I was not allowed on shore to post them myself and had to give them to him. She will have thought I had given up writing. I was desperate and could not understand why he did that.

That was the day before you came on board with the man with a cut arm and the girl. I was going to ask you to help me, but when I heard him, and that smarmy bloke talking of getting rid of you. I was terrified I would be got rid of as well. When the fireworks and the fight started I did not know what to do; if I helped you what would happen to

Ada? Then the cabin caught fire so I hid in the toilet until it was over. I was so glad you won and we went on the ferry and ashore. All Malloss said to me was keep quiet or Ada will suffer. But I want to be with Ada away from him. I hope I can get a ferry man to give this to you. Please, I beg you, help me. Please can you find out if Ada is OK without Malloss hurting her? You are my last hope.

Sorry to trouble you. Andy Hitchins

When he had finished reading it, Ellis said "Andy's story shows what an evil man Malloss is. Andy asks me for help to free them both and I am ready to do whatever I can for them whether or not it is in my interests too. We must find a way to do so."

Uncle John then explained "Andy's letter jogged my memory about Malloss. I have made enquiries, which confirm the details of the scandal at the Great Northern Bank a couple of years ago, when Malloss was chief executive. He made some serious errors and bad deals which nearly bankrupted the bank. The bad deals he made, so talk at the time suggested, were of a doubtful nature, even corrupt. But there appeared no evidence to link the deals to Malloss himself. As seems the norm these days, Malloss resigned under pressure, and walked away with a seven figure golden handshake.

"You might think there is no connection here to Malloss' attempt to sue you, but Andy's letter will ensure his past will come back to haunt him. This letter clearly explains the link between the deals that nearly destroyed the GNB, and Malloss.

"The situation for you, Ellis, as I see it, is this. PPP owns *Gaia Marina*; it is registered in its name. So the pursuer must be PPP. That means that the directors must agree to sue you at least by a majority. PPP has only three directors. Malloss, Simon Smith and Lady Malloss. She will vote to sue, doubtless as instructed by her husband. Assuming Simon as the second director refuses to agree to you being sued, on the face of it, Malloss can still sue you by 2 votes to 1. But as soon as Andy's letter is revealed to the authorities, demonstrating that the corrupt deals that cost the bank so dear were done by Malloss himself, his past denials will reinforce his guilt – he will be seen as lying.

"There are a lot of people who lost a lot of money in the scandal who will not hesitate to come down on Malloss like the proverbial ton of bricks, and from your point of view the result will be his disqualification to be a director. If he cannot be a director of PPP only Lady Malloss is left; Effectively PPP cannot sue you. You may be surprised that I make so much of this as you may think he could not possibly successfully sue you anyway, but there are risks in allowing the case to go to court. You did actually fire the rocket that set light to the cabin, and Malloss will say you stole the rocket too. That you were justified in doing so might not be regarded as relevant. Yes you would probably win, but how much better to avoid being taken to court in the first place.

"Incidentally Andy himself has nothing to fear from the law precisely because he could not have known what was in the paperwork he was delivering. Unfortunately however, he fears what Malloss will do to Ada long before the law catches up with him, and who can blame him?

"So we need to do two things; confirm Simon will vote against suing you, and we must remove the threat to Ada which prevents Andy from saying any more.

"Ellis, would you see Simon again? I would normally do so, but from your visit with Vaila I think you might be more likely to persuade him – or at least discover how he feels?"

"Certainly. I could go this evening. Although up to this morning I was in his eyes a bitter rival, he so appreciated Vaila's kindness that after she had left the room, he asked me to look after her . Yes I am happy to speak to him again about the vote.

"Vaila," said Uncle John,"how do you think Simon would react to Ellis?"

"I don't know, but of course, Ellis is the one being sued so it is logical that he should ask. I told Simon that I did not think we should meet again and I really want to stick to that for fear of opening wounds. Sorry Ellis, it is not a nice job for you to do. I could come as far as the hospital. Perhaps I could just see Inga and Mark? Then I would be in the wings to help if needed."

Uncle John continued, "If Simon meant what he said to you both it should be fine unless Malloss scares him. All you can do is try. Even if he abstained it might be enough."

"Next we must think about releasing Ada in Edinburgh, because it will only be when Andy and Ada are together and away from Malloss that we will feel free to use Andy's evidence. First, do you know anyone in Edinburgh who could confirm she is still at Malloss' house, Ellis?"

"Of course," said Ellis, "my Mum! She would think it a great game. None of Malloss' lot know her so there would be little risk that they would discover we were spying on the house."

"All she has to do is to attempt to discover if Ada is still in the house – no more. If she occasionally drove, or walked past the house, that might be enough. I wonder if Andy has a photo of her to help your Mother to identify her? Once we are sure she is still there you can work out what to do next."

"Right I will ring her. I can scan in a photo if Andy has one, and send it by E mail."

"Good. The next problem is that Ada does not know Andy is free, so will think she cannot rebel without him suffering. I cannot think how we could tell her. Without that, if we asked the police to try to release her she might actually refuse to leave for fear Andy would suffer. Besides, it would all take ages and we must get her before Malloss gets there and carries out his threat to hide her somewhere. As they all got bail this morning without any conditions there is nothing to stop Malloss going to Edinburgh so there is not much time to work out what to do and carry out the plan."

At this point Jean came into the office saying that Andy was back. Uncle John suggested he joined them and when he came in Vaila exclaimed "You look great in your new clothes Andy!" He beamed with pleasure. She thought it was probably the first time he had smiled in a long time.

Uncle John said "Andy, we were discussing how we could free Ada from Malloss' house as quickly as we can. Ellis' Mum lives in Edinburgh and Malloss does not know her so we are going to ask her to check Ada is still in the house. Have you a photo we could send her so she knows what Ada looks like?"

Andy pulled a small folder from his pocket and gave it to Ellis.

Thank you Andy it will only take a moment to scan it in to an Email to Mum and you can have it back. "

It took only five minutes to scan the photo, send it to Ellis' Mum together with Malloss' address which John found in the telephone book. Ellis returned the photo to Andy. He had also phoned her to be sure she got the message quickly.

Uncle John said to Andy "It is a bore for you, but I suggest you now stay in the flat until we know Malloss has left Orkney. It will probably be for a few days; we do not know how he will travel, but he must not know you are here, and now he is free to go where he wants he may be looking for you. It would be a disaster if he captured you before we have freed Ada."

Andy said "I am so grateful for your help. I did not know what to do. If only she could be here with me I would be glad to do all I can to help you stop him hurting anyone else. If he has hurt Ada....perhaps I should not say what I'd do if I could."

"Ellis," said Uncle John,"you indicated you had an idea?"

Ellis then outlined what he had in mind. The plan involved Vaila and himself going to Edinburgh, ahead of Malloss, and getting the help not only from his Mother but also his best friend Jeff when they were there.

"To prepare we need to get tickets to fly to Glasgow, as there is no direct Edinburgh flight. I will arrange it. We must give you, Andy, a mobile phone with all our numbers in it. Have you used one before?" Andy shook his head. "OK we will get one first thing tomorrow. We will show you how to use it, and you must practice so you know what to do without thinking because we may be in a hurry to reach you. When we do, we would hope to be with Ada, so that you could tell her who we are, and that we have come to rescue her. You will need to speak as briefly as you can as we may be in a hurry."

Andy said "Malloss told me that he intended to go to Edinburgh as soon as he could in the yacht to get it repaired and so he could move Ada to ensure she was absolutely safe in his care – so he said. He said that then I would never find her. I am worried he will murder her. Will he think I put you up to trying to get her back?"

Ellis replied "It is hard to know what he means Andy. What we know for certain is that he is an evil man. We need to get Ada away from his house before he gets there. We have to take a small risk to try to remove a far worse certainty. But we won't let you down Andy."

At that moment Ellis' mobile rang and he answered it. His Mother was very pleased with herself. She had driven past Malloss house as soon as she had got the photo, and had seen someone who she was sure was Ada at a window, cleaning an upstairs room. "She opened the window to shake a duster so I got a clear view." Janet MacKenzie reported.

"Thank you," said Uncle John, and Ellis passed on Uncle John's thanks and then listened again, laughed and said "I love you too Mum, you are definitely Scotland's answer to Sherlock Holmes!"

Malloss.

Ellis and Vaila arrived at the hospital at five, and found Inga on the reception desk. She said "Hello you two. You have arrived at a critical moment. Simon has a visitor, Malloss. As usual he was rude and demanding. Knowing what sort of a man he is I am surprised he takes any interest in visiting the sick."

Ellis looked alarmed, "I can guess what he has in mind. I will go in at once. Vaila, you go into the main ward to see Mark. Do not come out until either I call you or you have phoned Inga to ensure the coast is clear. I am afraid, Inga, we may have a confrontation, so if you have anyone acting as security warn them of possible trouble."

"I'm afraid we don't but at least we out number him."

He heard the end of an angry exchange from outside the door of Simon's single room "I will not sign and that is that. I have told you why, I haven't the energy to repeat it." Simon said.

Malloss was clearly furious. "You are a traitor to me, and for that matter to PPP. Our scheme can still work, still make us rich, but it is essential to sue MacKenzie for the good reasons I have explained. Are you too thick to understand? Are you too love sick to think straight? Have you surrendered that silly girl to MacKenzie without a proper fight? Don't be so weak. Are you scared of him or just soft in the head? Your reasons are not acceptable to me and I will have you drummed off the board unless you sign.

Ellis then marched into Simon's room without knocking. Malloss looked surprised, but his anger was if anything the worse for seeing Ellis. Simon was in a dressing gown in a chair beside the bed, on which was a sheet of paper and a pen –

presumably the document Malloss wanted Simon to sign. He looked relieved to see Ellis.

Malloss almost shouted at Ellis "So there you are. Yet another idiot I must deal with. You may have scared Simon witless over that damned girl but you must understand MacKenzie, you are going to pay for repairs to my yacht. You will also pay for the flares you wasted."

Ellis with some effort remained calm. "First, you will not describe Vaila as that damned girl in my presence. Second Simon is neither witless nor scared; on the contrary he shows great courage in sticking to his principles and promises regardless of whatever pressure you put him under. As for your plans to sue, we'll see, won't we?"

"You insolent puppy I'll take you for every penny you've got, then you will learn not to cross me, as you will soon find out. In the meantime get out of here, you are interfering in my plans yet again."

Ellis ignored him and asked Simon, "How are you feeling this evening?"

"I was doing fine but all this is not helping me. You might as well know what I am being asked. As Sir Frank just said, you will know one way or another soon enough anyway. He wants me to agree to you being sued in the name of PPP. Sir Frank deems it necessary to enable PPP to show it is doing all it can to protect it's charitable funds. He believes it is also right because you were the one that fired the rocket that caused the fire. But I do not agree. My feeling is that if we attempt to sue you in court, you are likely to defend yourself by..."

"Shut up," yelled Malloss, "you are giving away our case."

"Sir Frank, I do not think we have a case. I must ask that you listen. Nothing I say will be secret if we go to law. So as I was saying..."

"Shut up!"

"Very well, as Sir Frank does not want me to explain I will put it a different way. As you know Ellis, I made a promise to Vaila this morning, because she did me a big favour. What sort of a man am I if I abandon that promise only a few hours later? Not only that but I happen to think we would lose anyway if we sue, not only the legal case, but also substantial fees. I think I am making a rational decision in the interests of PPP. I am sorry to fall out with you, Sir Frank, but as a director I have a duty don't I to act according to my own judgment even if both the other directors do not like it. I hope you will come round to my way of thinking."

Ellis was astonished at Simon's little speech. He must have lain in bed through the day working it out in anticipation of Sir Frank's tirade, and now even Malloss was quiet for a moment or two. Then he tried again, this time in his quiet voice, just as he had on Gaia Marina.

"MacKenzie, you know perfectly well I am your superior in business and financial matters, and can run rings round you in any argument. So do not be deceived. You have not heard the last of all this. I hold a trump card. I do not suppose you know what it is, not even Simon does, but I shall use it before long. The effect will be to defeat all your 'noble' thoughts. Indeed we could well avoid a court case because you will be begging me to allow you to pay for the yacht plus much more beside. It will be a lesson to you for your insolence."

Ellis knew what he meant but was not going to give away that he knew. So he asked Simon "What is the paper you are supposed to sign?"

"My vote on the board to sue you." He looked straight at Ellis and added "There are three votes and my refusal makes the result 2-1 in favour, so my refusal to sign will not really make a difference, but I hope you will tell Vaila that I have made the only gesture available to me in keeping with my promise. I really appreciate what she did this morning."

Malloss butted in, "So MacKenzie you lose anyway. But I want a unanimous vote as a clear cut expression of solidarity."

Ellis replied "No Malloss, whatever cards you hold, you cannot win. You may perhaps win the odd victory but your inability to understand true loyalty and love will condemn you in the end. I would explain if I thought you would even listen."

Turning to Simon "Have you told Malloss what happened this morning?"

"No, that is part of my private life and I wish it to remain so. I know I can rely on Vaila and yourself to treat it in the same way. In any event it has had little influence on my decision to vote against suing you. Sir Frank thought I would be keen to sue you for taking Vaila from me. But you were right when you said the other day that you did not take her; she decided she wanted you, not me. She had every right to do so. I was disappointed, of course, but it is not your fault, or even hers. I made too many mistakes, so it was my own fault. Unfortunately Sir Frank does not agree as you heard."

"That is no way to win an argument." said Malloss harshly. "But I will not waste any more time here seeing I am amongst fools. But bear this in mind both of you. I will see you pay for the yacht, MacKenzie, and I will have you voted off the board of PPP, Simon without any compensation.

In the meantime I have to prepare Gaia Marina to sail to Edinburgh as soon as she is fit to go to sea. Thanks to you, MacKenzie, the trip may be uncomfortable but you will discover soon enough that you have lost."

As he moved towards the door Ellis wanted to provoke him into giving away when he would sail.

"You have not paid Euan and Mark. You are so mean I guess they will have to take you to the industrial court for it. But at least you might let them get their kit. I do see them from time to time; if you do not want to tell them can I at least tell them when they can get their stuff?"

"I do not know when we will sail as I do not know when she will be ready for sea. Maybe in three days? They had better not interfere with the work on her."

Ellis said "Andy's kit is also on board Euan could get that too if you know where he is to give it to him."

"No" interjected Malloss,"I want him to come to Edinburgh with me. I suppose none of your gang have seen him?"

Ellis said "No, I have not seen him since we were on your boat, I suppose he got bail too, so must have set out for home by himself."

"I doubt it. Nor do I think you would tell me if you do find him, but there's no good you looking for him,

MacKenzie, he is loyal to me – so you see I do understand loyalty."

"Do you? Anyway, I suppose I will next see you at the criminal trial." Malloss face gave away his fury at being reminded of that, but he said nothing; he just stormed out.

"Thank you, Ellis. Is Vaila OK?" said Simon.

"Fine, thank you. I will tell her what you said this evening; she will be grateful. I hope you will be fully recovered shortly. Good bye."

"I should be the grateful one. Her kindness will surely mean I won't suffer quite so long a sentence. Cheerio."

He spoke to Inga as soon as he returned to the reception area, who confirmed that Mark was fit to leave hospital. "Euan is coming to fetch him any time now. If you hang on a moment I expect you will see them both."

Right on cue, Euan walked in the door. "Hi it's good to see you. I hope Mark is ready; it's time to celebrate!"

"Good to see you too. It will save me a phone call." Ellis said "I have just had a conversation with Malloss, not a pleasant experience, but I did get him to agree you could go to Gaia Marina in St Margarets Hope to collect your things. There must be some folk working on her because he says he will set sail for Edinburgh as soon as she is fit to go to sea; he seems in a hurry but thinks it will be three days before she's ready. The poor man complained that with none of his lovely interior restored it might be uncomfortable!"

"Oh how sad! He passed me walking to the car park. Cut me dead, he did not even wish me good afternoon. He looked to be in a furious temper; what did you say to him?"

"I sort of told him off, because he was rude about Vaila. Then, believe it or not, Simon defied him too! So I supported Simon, as he was refusing to do what Malloss wanted him to do. First time I've done that but Simon is certainly a changed man, largely due to Vaila.

If you get the chance, let us know how he is getting on with the repairs to *Gaia Marina*. Incidentally, if you meet Malloss please do not give away that you have ever seen Andy, let alone that we know where he is. So if he wants you to take Andy's things just say there's no point you don't know where he is."

"Of course." Turning to Inga, Euan asked if Mark could now come with him. She told him "Mark was well enough to tease Hal and me so he is definitely well enough to leave!" She crossed the corridor opened the ward door and said to Mark, who was talking to Vaila, sitting on the nearest bed, "You can leave me in peace now, your friend awaits you, keen to celebrate."

Mark said to Ellis as soon as he stepped into the corridor "Did you know I've got a job on the Pentland ferry starting as soon as I am fit? I do not want to be hanging around so I shall start tomorrow morning, first thing" Ellis nodded.

"Good luck. It will be interesting to learn what the ferry crew thought of our adventure."

"I will get your kit from the yacht Mark," Euan said, "hopefully the last time I go aboard her." To Ellis he added "I've got a job on a rig, but do not start until next week. Incidentally I guessed you did not want Malloss to know that we met Andy."

"That must be a tightly guarded secret for now. I hope we will be in a position to bring this sorry mess to a conclusion and get rid of Malloss by this time next week. See you around. Come on Vaila we have things to do, and I must tell you of my little conversation with Sir Frank, the knighted devil himself."

As they drove home Ellis told her about his confrontation with Malloss, and the way Simon had stood up to the pressure Sir Frank had put him under. "Simon asked me, when Malloss had gone, to tell you he had done what he could to keep his promise to you. I said you would be grateful." "Yes I am, and doubtless you too. He really does sound as if he has turned over a new leaf. I wonder if he can keep it up, for his sake I hope so." She fell silent for a minute, and then asked.

"When you told Uncle John that Simon had asked you to look after me, this morning, you were about to add something else he had said to you, what was it?"

"Oh, nothing much."

Race and Rescue

The next morning Ellis rang to get tickets to fly to Glasgow. To his horror he was told that there were no available seats for the next four days. "It's the tourists, and some sporting fixtures as well as the usual business travellers I'm afraid." said the girl at the airline office.

He told Vaila and then suggested they book the ferry to go by car the next day. "We should still be in Edinburgh in good time. The real problem could be that my car is known to Malloss from the time we went to Peter and the Wolf. I remember seeing him as we parked the car, in the days when he wanted to be friendly. However, there does not seem to be much choice. I suggest we drive to Stromness to see Andy and buy the tickets at the pier office on the way back."

They were not even out of Kirkwall when there was a loud bang and the car stopped. Looking around it they could not see what was wrong, so Vaila rang Hal who said he had started work again as his arm was much better. He was on the way to a job, but he would come their way and see if he could sort it out. When he came it took him only a short time to identify the problem.

Ellis, not being at all mechanically minded, did not understand Hal's explanation, but understood all too clearly his summary. "You will need parts sent from the central belt before this can be repaired. It's a big job and I'm sorry Ellis, but the car will be off the road for several days. I can arrange with a friend to tow it to a garage for it to be sorted but I'm afraid you will need another way to get to Edinburgh in the meantime. Will you be able to continue with the trip?"

"We must. We cannot delay and, anyway, once we get to Edinburgh we can use my Mum's car. We just need to get there as soon as possible. Many thanks for getting the car to a garage. Can we stretch your assistance to taking us to Stromness?"

"Of course. I am trying to drive as much as I can to exercise this arm. Inga says I shouldn't but I am bored of doing nothing."

They were soon in Uncle John's office where they considered the problem. Discussing it there seemed only one possibility, to take the ferry on foot and then go by train or bus to Inverness and then to Edinburgh again by train or bus.

"It's a slow journey that way, effectively over two days." Ellis thought that it still ought to get them to Edinburgh before Malloss had got *Gaia Marina* in a fit state to go to sea, assuming it would take him three days. Malloss would then need around 48 to 60 hours sailing to get there.

It was as if his phone had read his thoughts, and its ring had a taste of urgency about it. When Ellis answered it, he heard Euan on the phone. "Ellis you really have a problem now. *Gaia Marina* has gone!"

"What do you mean – has she actually gone to sea?"

"Yes. Gone to sea. Mark told me about it just now. I did not tell him it was vital you got to Edinburgh first and needed to know if *Gaia Marina* had left, because we thought it would be several days before she could sail. So he only told me when he came off the morning ferry sailing. I would not have known then but he joked about seeing her not far from where our little battle was. She must have left early this morning. I'm so sorry, I feel we have let you down."

"That's OK, but I must see what we can do now. Thanks, must go." He put the phone down and gave Vaila and Uncle John the news.

"What can we do now?" Asked Vaila in a despairing voice.

Uncle John said "Time to see if we can do something special. It may not work but we must try. Would you go and see Andy? Do not alarm him with Euan's news, but tell him you are preparing to leave for Edinburgh. Ensure he has mastered the mobile and reassure him. He must use my phone if he wants to get a message to you, so he keeps his available night and day for your call. Now off you go. Come back in about 15 minutes."

When they returned to his office he said, "We are in luck. I have spoken to Tom Triscoll, and when I explained the problem he just asked what he could do to help.

I asked if there was any chance that you could use the company private jet. Unfortunately it is in Norway at the moment but he does have an Islander on the Flotta airstrip and he was planning to use it to go to Edinburgh tomorrow anyway. The pilot is not available until then, but if we can work out what time you would have to leave to beat Malloss, then he does not mind how early you need to take off in the morning. There is, of course, light from about 4am at this time of year."

With a map and details of weather and distance, together with Euan's estimate of *Gaia Marina's* speed they worked out that they needed to be in Edinburgh no later than noon the following day. This was put to the pilot over the phone, and the decision was made and the arrangements put in place.

Hal would take Vaila and Ellis to Houton Pier by 6 in the morning, where the company launch would meet them and take them across to Flotta. Tom would meet them, take them to the airstrip and the aircraft would take off no later than 7. Their flight time to Edinburgh would be about 3 to 4 hours, to arrive about 11.00 which would allow a little time to spare in case their calculations were wrong. Janet MacKenzie would meet them. It ought to enable them to have around an hour or two to get Ada. Ellis feared that there were too many steps where delays might occur, but it was the only plan that stood a chance of working. He did not want to suggest an earlier start, feeling that would be stretching Tom Truscoll's generosity too far, just to quieten his own impatience.

Ellis' alarm went off at 4.30 am. He quickly shaved and dressed, ensured that he had everything he might need for the trip in his pockets, roughly made the bed and went along the landing as quietly as he could.

He knocked on Vaila's door and softly called, "Are you awake?" to which she called "Yes. You go down to the kitchen and put the kettle on. I'll be with you in a minute." Ellis was about to knock on Hal's door when he came out, so they went down stairs together.

"Good Morning. I wish I was coming with you but anyway I hope it goes well."

"I expect so. After all I will have your feisty sister to keep me right."

Vaila joined them for their brief breakfast five minutes later, and as they cleared up he saw her as he had seen her on his working visit. She was wearing the same sweater and jeans as she had worn when meeting him at the airport when he had arrived on that occasion. Was it really only six weeks ago? But it was more than that. Now he also saw her as his girlfriend. He realised he was becoming more than a little fond of her.

She stopped his reverie. "Come on Ellis, what are we waiting for?"

"Just anticipating another adventure with my fellow adventurer. Let's roll then."

There was a slight chill in the early morning air, but it was clear, bright and still as they walked out to Hal's car. Ellis felt as if they were going on a secret mission. No one would know they had gone and he felt excited by the prospect as he anticipated a memorable day, not least as it seemed the perfect weather for it.

They arrived promptly at the Houton ferry pier just as the company launch from Flotta was coming in, exactly as planned and arranged by Tom Triscoll. They met him at the Gibraltar pier on Flotta and joined him in his car. He said, "Good morning folks. A great morning for a race and a rescue I guess? I hope it will all work out for you all."

The Islander was awaiting them at the airstrip and they immediately climbed in as the pilot directed them. He told them that the plane was so noisy that he would have to give the safety briefing before starting up. He explained that, although he could talk to Tom Triscoll, who was sitting in the seat normally occupied by a co-pilot, through the head sets, Vaila and Ellis would just have to guess what he had to say once airborne.

It was just 6.30 and the pilot was just about to start the engines when he stopped. He acknowledged a radio message, and said "I expect so. I'll radio back in a few moments."

He turned to Ellis and Vaila; Triscoll had already heard the message through the earphones, "We have been asked to take a child and his mother to Kirkwall; the child has been taken seriously ill in the night. They will be here in a minute or two. Is that OK?"

Triscoll "Said it's up to you folks; I am in no hurry."

Ellis and Vaila looked at each other then Ellis said "Of course, but could you radio Kirkwall and tell them we are on an errand of mercy too, so can they arrange for there to be no delay there?"

By the time the pilot had radioed the message, Vaila saw a car approaching. It came quite close to the aircraft. The pilot asked the two of them to move to the very back seats, to make it easier for the mother, who was carrying her child in a blanket, to get in quickly and easily.

Islander aircraft have no aisle; each set of two seats is reached by its own door. To Ellis It seemed an age before everyone was strapped in, but at last the engines were started and they took off. They were given priority to land at Kirkwall Airport but when they taxied up to the terminal there was another short delay whilst the ambulance was brought as near as practicable so that the child and his mother could be transferred. They then had to wait whilst another incoming flight landed, during which time the pilot asked Ellis and Vaila to move back to their original seats, and by the time they had taken off and set a course southward it was already nearly nine o'clock.

Ellis spoke into Vaila's ear against the noise "We are now nearly two hours later than I had hoped. But we could not have refused the diversion. I hope my Mum is in a good place to pick us up, as it is going to be a close run thing to get to Malloss' house before he does."

She replied "How sure are you of the time Malloss will be there?"

"Not at all sure. I just hope all our arrangements will work as planned. If not we will have to be inventive. But it may be impossible to get Ada out if Malloss gets there first as he knows us. We would lose the advantage that Lady M does has not met us. But there is nothing we can do about it at the moment."

But he felt anxious and impatient and just could not relax. He had the absurd wish to push at the seat in front of him to make the aircraft fly faster. He must have somehow given away the tense knot in his stomach, for he felt Vaila's hand on his and saw her smile at him and for a while he was soothed by her presence.

As the aircraft flew down the coast of Caithness in the bright light of a pleasant summer's morning Ellis could pick out a number of landmarks. For something to do he pointed out each to Vaila. Wick harbour and the streets around it were laid out like a map. A few minutes later Dunbeath Castle was below, dramatically perched on what seemed no more than a pinnacle of rock on the edge of the cliff above the sea. A slight change of course to the east took them over the sea. They soon saw Fraserburgh and Peterhead to the left of the aircraft as they crossed the Buchan coast. The pilot maintained their course which once more took them over the coast near Ellon. By 11.15 they were passing Aberdeen, which they saw to their right around five miles away as the pilot had to avoid traffic at Dyce airport. They could just make out the movement of helicopters as they flew under them on their way to the North Sea rigs, and in the far distance they could just see one or two of the rigs themselves.

It was just after noon by the time they had crossed Fife reaching the Firth of Forth near Leven. The pilot then turned sharply westward, following the Fife coast. All the time they had been over the sea they had looked out for a yacht but had seen only fishing boats and a few supply vessels.

Then, as Ellis looked out of the port side window, he saw a large yacht passing Inchkeith Island. It looked as if she was turning to port presumably to enter the lock into Leith dock. He was reasonably sure it was *Gaia Marina* by her rig and colour. He wondered how long it would take her to go through the lock, and to tie up so that Malloss could go ashore. For that matter would Malloss, if he looked up and saw the aircraft, guess or even know it had come from Orkney?

As they had had to fly via Kirkwall could they have been seen by someone who could radio the yacht? Maybe he would think it was an ambulance flight? It did not really matter, but he wondered if Malloss could he see the insignia of the company on the side of the aircraft. Speculation was pointless; they were in a race to get to Malloss' house in time to effect a rescue of Ada before Malloss arrived and it was impossible to know who was winning at that point.

Ellis saw that they were lining up for their final approach to the airport when the pilot increased engine speed suddenly and started to climb. He could not explain to those in the back because of the noise of the aircraft so Ellis could only fret at the delay. They crossed the airport and started a long circuit around it. In spite of his growing concern at the delay, he could admire the magnificent view of the bridges across the Forth at Queensferry as they banked over them. Then they turned again to approach the runway once more.

At long last they touched down at Edinburgh airport and taxied to the stand for private aircraft. Ellis thanked the pilot as soon as the engines were switched off, who said "Sorry for the extra circuit. Air traffic Control sent us round again as an aircraft on the ground had engine problems on the runway. It could not take off as planned so we had to do a circuit while it was sorted out."

Ellis thanked Tom Triscoll who replied "My pleasure. Good luck I hope you make it. I'll want to hear all about it when we get home! I am sorry I cannot offer a lift back but I doubt if I will be finished in time to return today."

As they had no luggage to deal with they ran through the terminal to the pickup area where Ellis' Mum was waiting with the car. The moment she saw them she got out and said to Ellis "You drive. As I am meeting Vaila for the first time, we'll sit in the back. I am keen to get to know her after all you have told me about her. We can talk about you while you drive."

"You see Vaila, even my Mum teases me. Oh how I suffer!"

As Ellis set off he heard his Mum say to Vaila "It is so good to meet you Vaila. I have heard a lot about you and your adventures. But you know what men are. I suspect he hasn't told me the half of it."

Fifteen minutes later, Ellis said "OK you should keep the record of my childhood until later, Mum. Time to concentrate on today's adventure."

By the time they had settled on their tactics they were approaching the Braid Hills district where Malloss' large house was.

Ellis asked; "Mum, direct me so we pass the house, and we'll park as near as we can but out of sight of it."

The house, or as Vaila saw it, the mansion, was on their right in a quiet, elegant street. Only 50 meters or so beyond it Ellis turned left into a side street. Luckily there was a space to park near the corner.

"Right girls, let's start plan A. Before we get out I will turn round. I will leave the key in the car so there will be no delay should we need a quick getaway."

They approached the house together. Ellis noticed that on the left side of the house, as they approached it, was a passage leading round to the back. It had a solid door, but it was ajar. On the right side was a garage reached by a drive about two cars length long.

As planned Janet knocked on the front door. It was opened a young girl, dressed as a maid, who asked them what they wanted.

"Good Morning, my dear," said Janet "we are from the local church and are collecting for the organ fund. Would the lady of the house be nearby?"

A voice from behind the maid called "Who is it?"

"From the Church M'lady it's about the organ."

"What? Oh, I had better deal with it."

The maid disappeared and Lady Malloss came to the door. Somehow she looked just as Ellis would have expected. Thin – too thin. He had a fleeting vision of kipper bones, but managed to keep a straight face. She was certainly well-dressed, but the effect was spoilt by a sour expression.

"What do you want?"

"We are from the church, collecting for the organ. It needs repair and we can only do it if we raise the money. Will you help?"

"No. Is that all?"

"One other thing. We understand that you have a past member of the church working for you. We have not seen her for some time so we thought we would ask if we could speak to her. Her name is Ada Hitchens."

"Certainly not. My husband is very strict about to whom our staff speak. He is due home any minute so I suppose you could try again later, but I do not think he would agree. Perhaps she no longer wants to go to church."

"It would only take a moment, so we can reassure her friends in the church she is well?"

"No, she is busy and I do not want her distracted from her duties. Anyway, I cannot call her as she is putting out the washing at the back. Please go. Good bye." She shut the door in their faces.

Ellis said quietly. "Back to the car Mum. Start it and bring it to the corner where you can see us. If we beckon come and pick us up. We'll go looking as planned. We may be in luck as it could be easier to extract her from the garden than from within the house."

As Janet returned to the car, Vaila and Ellis went round to the side door they had seen, being careful to remain below the window they passed. Going through the door Ellis was careful to put it back as if closed and they quickly walked round to the back. When they got to the corner of the house they could see the whole of the back garden, mostly a very large neatly cut lawn. On the far side was a man working on a flower bed. There was a slabbed area outside a French window with tables and chairs. To their left, against the garden wall was a small stone and tiled lean-to garden building and just visible on the other side of it, the end of a washing line could be seen. They had to walk past the small building to see beyond it properly and were relieved to see a woman hanging up washing from a large basket. Vaila immediately went up to her as Ellis took out his mobile, and dialled a pre-set number.

Vaila smiled and said to the woman "Hello, are you Ada Hitchens?"

She looked startled "Er yes, who are you?" as she spoke she looked around nervously as if to be sure no one could see her.

"My name is Vaila Flett, this is Ellis MacKenzie. We have come to fetch you." As she spoke Ellis' phone was answered by Andy.

"Ellis here, as planned Andy, we are with Ada but we think Malloss is not far behind us. Here is Ada. Remember to reassure her we are who we say we are. We will need to be quick." He said to Ada, "here is Andy on the phone. He will explain very briefly that he is free and we need to get you away from here as fast as we can." He handed the phone to Ada.

She said "Is that really you Andy?" A pause while she listened. She smiled, and tears started to run down her cheeks.

"Yes its Vaila Flett and Ellis MacKenzie. We are still in the garden of Malloss' house. They say Malloss will be here any moment."

She listened again. "I love you too. I'm longing to see you."

Ellis held his hand out to take the phone. He took it and said "Well done Andy. We'll keep in touch. We'll ring again when we are sure we are safe; good bye."

"Andy says I am to do whatever you tell me. That you are taking me to him. Thank you, thank you." She wept with happiness.

"We must go, Ada." said Vaila putting her hand on Ada's arm.

"Can I just get my things?"

"No, you must come right now as you are. We can get your stuff later." Ellis rather doubted it, but he wanted no delay.

Vaila took her hand. They started to return the way that they had come in, but when they reached to door at the side of the house they heard a car draw up.

"Put the car in the drive." The voice was instantly recognisable, it was Malloss. He walked swiftly to the front door, took out a key and opened it. As he did so he shouted "Joanna. Joanna – ah there you are. Is all well?"

Ellis could not hear the reply but before Malloss shut the door they heard him ask "Have there been any callers this morning? I think those blasted idiots from Orkney may try something. Now get that woman Hitchens, I must take her to..." The door slammed shut and Ellis could hear no more.

"Quick lets go. Come on." He led Ada and Vaila quickly on to the pavement and waved to his Mum, who immediately drove out of the side street, in front of a passing car who hooted her, and pulled up beside them.

"Quickly – Vaila and Ada in the back." He opened the door for them and shut it as soon as they were in, jumped into the front passenger seat, shut the door and said "Drive Mum – anywhere for now."

As he did so the front door of the house was flung open and Malloss yelled "Stop. How dare you. Stop. Robbers. Thieves. Stop."

Two neighbours opposite, who were in the front gardens of their houses looked up, but Ellis' last glimpse of them suggested that they were not in a hurry to help Malloss. Vaila turned to look out of the back window, and saw Malloss run to his car, a large estate, inevitably green she felt, push his chauffeur aside and get in. She saw no more as Janet turned left at the end of the road.

"I think he is after us." said Vaila.

"So long as he does not get ahead of us I am not sure what he can do." Replied Ellis. "Mum remember to keep to the speed limit, and, let's all get seat belts on. It would not help to get stopped by the police."

"Do you think Malloss will ring them to ask that we are stopped for hi-jacking Ada?"

"No, he would be mad to do that. After all, he is on bail for several crimes already. Let's see what he does for now. So long as we stay on streets with people and other vehicles I guess all he can do is discover where we are going."

"He may have other men like Sid and Bill around, do you think?"

"I do not know. But he has not had time to organise anything elaborate. Of course if he guesses we are going back to Orkney he might be able to arrange for us to be intercepted somewhere. His first guess is likely to be that we will drive north. He may well be able to arrange something because there is only one main road all the way to Gills Bay or Scrabster. I think our two best options are to go to Glasgow to catch a flight in the morning, or to get the train to Aberdeen from where we can get a ferry to Lerwick, and then back to Orkney. It's a long way round but he would surely only think of that if he knew we were heading for Aberdeen.

Whatever we choose, the first thing we need to do is to lose him here, so he does not know what we are doing. It's time for reinforcements!"

Ellis rang Jeff; "Hi Jeff it's Ellis with another problem!"

Pause "So sorry to drag you into a car chase, I know how you hate excitement, you poor old thing!" and he laughed. "Hang on, I had better explain to the others what's going on here."

He turned to the back seat so Vaila and Ada could hear him "In spite of what you heard, Jeff is as usual longing to have a go at Malloss. His Dad suffered when the GNB nearly crashed due to that man. He also loves cars! I count Jeff as my best friend."

216

He turned back to the phone "I trust you are hanging on to my every word still?" pause, "Ha ha! Did you get that bright red Corsa you had your eyes on?"

"Great then it's just like Mum's car so we can lead Malloss astray."

Ellis listened. "That sounds perfect. We were debating whether to get a train to Aberdeen and then a ferry or to go to Glasgow airport for the first flight tomorrow. Whichever we do we need to lose him in Edinburgh. Edinburgh airport might be possible, it will confuse him no end because he must know there are no direct flights to Kirkwall from there. That should increase the chances of losing him."

He listened again to Jeff's next suggestion.

"Yes I can see that would be the easiest way to do it. We will ring when we are in position. We'll all fit in OK. Much appreciated mate, I'll owe you a pint."

Short pause "Why not, it's a deal. See you shortly." Ellis laughed and rang off.

Turning to the others, he explained what Jeff had suggested, and ended by saying that he had promised Jeff a bottle of Highland Park if they could pull off the plan.

"Right Mum, first we are going to switch cars. We may be able to lose him by fooling him into following the wrong car. After that we have two other ideas including going to Edinburgh Airport. Is Malloss still with us?"

She looked in the mirror and replied "Yes, three cars behind.

" Let's lead him a dance, as we have to waste a bit of time so Jeff can get in position. Let's start by going to Waverly station. "

"You can't go into it anymore. "

"Yes I know, just go to the Market Street entrance. Turn next right and then left on to St Leonard's and the Pleasance. Then straight across the Royal Mile. After that take the next left. The station entrance is then just in front of us. Let's see if the lights will enable us to play tricks. "

The lights did as Ellis hoped. At the Royal Mile they got through just as they were turning red, so Malloss was delayed until the lights went green again. Janet stopped the car where they would be dropped off for the station. Ellis, Vaila and Ada ducked down so they could not be seen from another car unless it was very close, and when Janet saw Malloss come round the corner behind several cars, she moved off, waving out of the window as if she had dropped her passengers. It worked; Malloss also stopped and got out of his car, as Janet reached the roundabout at the end of the street and turned right towards Princes Street.

Malloss was not fooled for long, although he was delayed crossing the road, once he was in the station entrance he could have seen them on the passenger bridge, had they been there. By this time, of course, Ellis could not see him, but when they were held up by the Princes Street lights, Vaila saw him coming round the roundabout rather faster than was sensible. He was only four cars behind them when the lights turned green. But the manoeuvre demonstrated Malloss' determination, and Ellis suspected it was anger that led him to be so keen to confront them.

"Go to Castle Street next, Mum. Along Princes Street and right."

"When they were stopped at the next traffic light, Ellis said, "How are you getting on with the hands free phone?"

"It's great, except it's so tempting to phone everyone that it's getting expensive!"

"The main thing is that once we have transferred to Jeff's car we may still need to communicate with you. We will want to be sure you are OK with that evil man following you."

They crossed George Street as Malloss was just turning into Castle Street, but they saw that once he got to George Street he might be held up.

"OK Mum, turn left into Young street and stop at the entrance to the lane. Turning to the back he said "Ready, we need to get out as fast as we can and down the lane. Take your belts off now. Ready?"

Both Ada and Vaila confirmed they were ready, and as Janet turned into Young Street, Ellis could see Jeff turning into Castle Street from Queen Street. So as arranged he rang Jeff's number, let in ring three times, and cut the call, but he thought Jeff had seen them anyway.

Ellis had his door open and was out of the car in seconds and was glad to see Vaila had almost been as quick. Ada had to slide across the back seat so was a second or two later. They slammed the doors and Janet immediately set off as they scrambled down the lane. They just got to the corner when they saw Malloss pass in pursuit of Janet's car. As soon as he had gone Ellis said, "here we go back to Young Street."

Jeff came round the corner a moment later. He had been lucky to make the right turn without having to wait for traffic so that they were in his car in a few seconds. Vaila was in front this time, as Ellis left the navigation to Jeff.

"That was great, Malloss has gone in pursuit of Mum. I think she turned right down North Charlotte Street."

Jeff went round Charlotte Square at a sedate pace, trying to look as cool as he could.

He said "Hello, everybody. What a lovely day for a chase around. I will go out to Barnton. If Malloss finds us there we have the option of heading north or to Glasgow for plan B – or is it C? If that fails to stop him there is always the Edinburgh airport option. It might be easier to lose him there with so many folk, and traffic."

As they drove past Daniel Stewarts School, Jeff turned to Vaila, and said

"So you're the famous Vaila."

"I think I must be; there is no other Vaila in the car! How come you think me famous?"

"Ellis was supposed to spend some of his hols with his old friends in Edinburgh. Several times I E mailed him, so I did, and there was always some excuse that he could not come. First it was the festival, then it was a new find, and then it was something else so I guessed it was a girl. Under threat of whatever I could think of he finally confessed, and told me all sorts of nice things about you. He certainly thinks you are famous, and now I've met you I fully understand why he could not tear himself away from Orkney!"

In a louder voice to be sure Ellis could hear, "But Vaila, what on earth do you see in our dusty old archaeologist?

What you need to look after you in Auld Reekie is a bright guy like me!"

Ellis from the back laughed "Jeff, hands off or I'll tell Liz."

"Oh, you can't do that, it's sneaking."

"Vaila, take no notice of Jeff, he has to try, but Liz keeps him in line." And the two friends burst out laughing.

"Tell me about Liz, then." Jeff smiled and said, "If I have to be serious – not an easy thing for me – she's my girl and I love her to bits, but we enjoy ragging each other, and when Ellis joins in I usually lose, but maybe I might win occasionally if you are going to be around to be my ally!"

Vaila was thinking of her response, and revelling in the assumption that she really might be coming to Edinburgh again with Ellis, when Ellis' phone rang.

"Hi, Tom here. How did your mission go Ellis?"

"Entirely successful, but we are just evading Malloss who saw us making off with Ada and has been following us around. I think we have lost him."

He looked over his shoulder only to see what he was sure was Malloss half a dozen cars behind, so he added, "Oh no. I think he has found us again."

"Well you guys, my meetings have finished much more quickly than I thought, so I have decided to return this evening. If you can lose Malloss and haven't fixed a return journey would you like a lift?"

"Wonderful, yes we would, it is so kind of you to offer. Three of us now of course. When do you want us?"

"Can you make the private aircraft lounge OK, in around 30 to 45 minutes?"

"We will do our damnedest. That is really great, marvellous. Thank you so much."

When Ellis had explained the phone call, Jeff said' "I think there is a separate drop- off for those going on private aircraft but I have no idea where it is. It's bound to be at the far right side of the main terminal somewhere, that's where the private aircraft stand. I think I will have to go into the main car park to drop you off. We can't go round and round looking with Malloss on our tail. What do you think?"

"Mum picked us up there this morning but the main drop off would probably be best anyway because there are always dozens of people milling around. He would be mad to tackle us there."

"Yes, but I think he is a bit mad anyway. So what I will do is to park rather than just drop you off. I can then come with you as far as the lounge in support."

"That would be great. Thanks, Jeff."

Jeff drove into the short stay multi-storey car park at the airport. It was fairly full and there were other cars going round, either looking for a space or leaving. He found a space in the middle of a row on the first floor and nipped into it. He was not quite sure if Malloss had come into that section of the car park.

"OK jump out, but watch for Malloss."

"You lead Jeff, then Ada and Vaila, and I will be behind you." He whispered to Vaila, "keep close to Ada, she will not know the way and is probably nervous."

They got out of the car, and as the clearly marked exit from the car park was beyond three rows of cars, Jeff led them between the immediate row to the road beyond, saw no cars and said, "Straight ahead, whilst there are no cars coming."

Jeff Ada and Vaila got between the next row of parked cars and Ellis was crossing the roadway when Malloss came round the end of the road. He saw Ellis, and drove at him at full speed. He jumped back and just made it between the first row cars, but caught his foot and fell against one of them and on to his knees. Malloss screeched to a stop, leapt out and yelled at him "Come here you bastard! Now I've got you; you cannot get out, that exit it is locked!"

Jeff had just reached it and indeed found it locked; a notice on the door marked with an arrow said "This way to exit." He took Ada in the direction indicated, but Vaila, seeing Ellis picking himself up, and Malloss running to him, ran back as fast as she could to help Ellis, unsure if he had been hurt when he fell.

She had just reached Ellis when Malloss, just behind her, viciously knocked her aside and, in the moment when Ellis was getting up, kicked him. He then immediately turned round to Vaila again, now just behind him, and grabbed her wrist.

But the kick had been ineffectual. Ellis, back on his feet, saw Malloss trying to pull Vaila towards his car. She however resisted so strongly, pulling back, hitting him with her free hand and attempting to kick him, that he let go of her and pushed her on to the bonnet of the nearest car. She could not help but cry out in pain.

Ellis, now face to face with Malloss, was so angry with him for attacking and hurting Vaila that he gave no thought for anything else. He punched Malloss in the face as hard as he could.

Malloss stopped in his tracks and for a moment stared at Ellis, as if he could not quite believe what Ellis had done.

"Punishment for your insolence to Vaila."

Malloss felt his nose as it started to bleed profusely.

"Damn you. I'll get you for this. I'll teach you not to do that to your betters." He spat the words out at Ellis but he could do or say no more. He had to put a handkerchief to his face to stop the blood from his nose running down his face.

As Malloss turned and returned to his car, re-starting it, Ellis turned to Vaila,

"Are you OK?"

"I'm fine, just glad he didn't get me to his car. I didn't fancy being captured by him a second time. He won't forget your punch! Again you have rescued me! Thank you." She laughed.

"Quickly then, to the exit," said Ellis.

Malloss saw what they intended and wanted to try again. If he could get to the roadway alongside the wall beyond the final two rows of cars he would be able to drive at them again. Jeff said to Ellis, "I'll get the girls to the exit, staying on the side of these parked cars so we can get between them if necessary. Come on."

But then suddenly it was over. Malloss, determined to get to the next roadway, had to back to the point where he could do so. But he was so focused on his revenge, and so angry that he did not look at what he was doing. He accelerated backwards as fast as he could straight into a Range Rover looking for a parking space. It was a noisy crash, and a final one.

As the furious Range Rover driver got out, Jeff quietly called Ellis, who had turned to look,

"Come on. Let's go. He can sort himself out. I'll see you into the terminal. With any luck Malloss will be gone by the time I come back to get my car to go home."

They were through the exit door, down the stairs and heading for the private flight lounge when Ellis said quietly "Ow!"

Vaila looked at him walking beside her, "What is it?"

"My hand hurts. That man has a hard head."

"Once we are on the plane, I'll kiss it better - my hero!" She smiled at him.

He then spoke to Ada. "Are you OK? It wasn't meant to be like this."

She replied exitedly. "I feel wonderful! I've never had such an exciting time before! I loved it when you hit Malloss, I'll remember that for ever!"

In the lounge they met Tom Triscoll. He asked how they had managed to evade Malloss.

"A closer encounter than planned and we had a final confrontation with him in the car park. But here we all are and that's the main thing. It is so kind of you to think of us. After all that has happened today, never mind the early start, I think I will sleep all the way home!"

"Good, well we are ready to go. I intend landing in Kirkwall, and the pilot suggests we will be landing around 6 this evening. Anything you need?"

"Yes," said Ellis, "although doubtless Vaila will tease me about it, but I'm hungry. Once again we had no lunch!"

"Andy's just the same." Said a very cheerful Ada.

"It's all free in the lounge" laughed Tom. "Help yourself."

Vaila handed Ada the phone, "Your turn. I've dialled Andy, so you can tell him the good news and that we are on our way. Perhaps he will meet us."

They then went out to the aircraft.

Conclusion

Just after 6 pm the aircraft taxied to the stand by the Kirkwall terminal, and the pilot switched off the engines. Vaila gently removed Ellis' head from her shoulder where it had been for most of the trip, as he slept. As he stirred she said "Wakey, wakey, sleepy head."

Ellis yawned. "I do not remember much of that flight. Did you manage to sleep yourself?"

"Yes, most of the way and in spite of the noise, we slept together. Oh dear I better not say that to Mum, it might be misinterpreted!" She laughed.

They all walked to the terminal building and as they went Ellis found himself thanking Tom and the pilot for the second time that day. The whole family were there to meet them. Andy could not wait. He ran forward as soon as he saw Ada to embrace her. They clung to each other in sheer joy.

"That makes it all worthwhile doesn't it?" said Vaila watching them and feeling quite emotional herself. She put her arm round Ellis to match her feelings.

The family were full of questions, just as Vaila and Ellis were full of the day's adventure and after they had given a brief account of the rescue, Uncle John asked, "I expect you will want a lie in tomorrow, so why don't we all have a party tomorrow evening? I shall get some champagne and then I will tell you all that has happened since you rang to say you had successfully rescued Ada. Malloss really is in deep water now.

He turned to Andy and Ada and said "It is inevitable that the police want to interview you tomorrow, and after a nights rest you will probably be happy to get that behind you, so I have arranged for the police to come to the office about 11. If you want to leave it for a while I am sure they will agree, as they have much of the story from the letter you sent to Ellis. I gave it to them as soon as I knew Ada was safely on the plane."

The two A's were happy to fall in with anything suggested by Uncle John. He continued "It will be a busy day because as soon as the police have completed the interview, I intend to ring Malloss' lawyer. Now that there is so much evidence against him he really has little chance of avoiding a serious prison sentence and in my view no chance at all of successfully suing you.

"Surely Malloss will withdraw the action now. I would expect his legal team to advise him to concentrate on how to minimize the considerable compensation he will have to pay to you Vaila, and of course Hal, Mark, and most of all, Andy and Ada."

Ellis replied, "I would not bank on his withdrawing any claim against me, because when he confronted us in the airport car park, he hurt Vaila. I just could not let him do that. It made me so angry that I hit him as hard as I could, and may well have broken his nose. He said he'd sue me for it."

The family cheered at that news, and even Uncle John smiled and said "Serve him right! It must surely be a clear case of your defending Vaila! Not quite what a lawyer should say but never mind. If he did sue he would make himself the laughing stock of his own circle as well as the general public, never mind all those who lost money. You would become quite a celebrity!"

It proved a great party. Uncle John had invited all the family and everyone who had helped including Tom Triscoll, Mark and Euan, and of course, Andy and Ada.

Uncle John said, "Just before we open the well-deserved Champagne let me tell you how I got on today.

I rang Malloss' lawyers once the police finished the interview. I told them that although Malloss had indicated that he wished to sue my clients in PPPs name for the costs of repairing the yacht, it was my duty to inform them that several of my clients would be suing him, personally, for substantial damages under a number of headings. They started to say that Malloss particularly wanted to see Mr. MacKenzie being sued for every last penny, including for assaulting him.

I told them very firmly that the results of the criminal charges, both for his corrupt practices at the GNB, and for all that happened on the yacht, never mind Malloss and his wife's imprisonment of Andy and Ada would I believe make it unlikely that he could successfully sue for anything. I asked if they were aware that the police were in possession of written evidence which would be extremely difficult to deny. They sounded as if they were not. Malloss seems to have told them nothing if I have interpreted their reaction correctly.

I was especially determined that Andy and Ada should receive a considerable sum for being in effect enslaved. The lawyers sounded very unhappy to hear about that issue.

Naturally they told me nothing but their silence seemed to me to give a lot away. They said they would consult their client.

Later they rang back. I have no idea what they said to Malloss, of course, but they told me that he had decided to withdraw all claims against all of my clients. I said I was pleased to hear it, but I could not reciprocate. I did however suggest that it might be possible to persuade my clients to negotiate an out of court settlement. I think they will recommend that to their client. It means that Malloss has unconditionally surrendered, and that it just remains to negotiate terms.

That still leaves the question of the purpose of the bomb on the fence and indeed of PPP. I have enquired of OSCAR – the charity regulator – to discover that the statutory returns that PPP submitted to them, seen in the light of the evidence you have given, suggest that PPP have collected a lot of donations, and a sizable reclaim of tax from Gift Aid. I then discovered that most of their so called lobbying was with other genuine NGOs such as the two National Trusts, and Treasures of Scotland. Malloss offered PPP staff to work with their membership departments without cost, saying that it would help PPP's campaign against pollution. All these bodies were suspicious, and declined. They were right to do so. We may never know but I suspect Simon's charm, persuasiveness and his computer skills were to be used to get into their membership records, which is why Malloss wanted to employ him. It is lucky for Simon he was never in a position to exercise those skills, so at least he escapes any prosecution in that regard.

PPPs expenditure seems limited to administration costs, salaries including to Malloss himself, and quite a lot of travel costs, mainly to interesting places, such as tax havens. They may well have a good story about how this was necessary but I could not begin to guess what it could be. In the detailed accounts there are also other items that require explanation. OSCAR were honest enough to say that they had not looked at the accounts in detail until now. Once OSCAR and other authorities start digging around I suspect things may become even more uncomfortable for PPP and its President. Incidentally Simon was a director of PPP too, although he has resigned in the last few days. He will therefore get some of the blame should PPP be revealed as having broken charity law, but Malloss will be considerably more troubled by it.

He will try to get credit for giving PPP the yacht, but it is unlikely to help him, as he has continued to use it as his own. We will see what develops but Malloss is cornered; all you have to do is to appear as witnesses, if required.

Ellis was looking very happy "I do hope that means yet more court cases will be held in Orkney!"

Uncle John laughed "Not all of them Ellis, but you do not need excuses to come; one Orcadian will welcome you with open arms at any time."

Vaila tried not to blush, and nearly succeeded.

"One last thing; you were absolutely right Ellis about PPP. Malloss was never interested in bombing the Oil terminal, or pollution. He just wanted the publicity a minor attack on the fence might give him. All along the objective of PPP was to garner money from donations, membership, gift aid and by selling membership lists of other NGOs. If it had worked, and they had got away with it, then as Simon boasted to Vaila, he would have become rich and Malloss would have become even richer than he was from the GNB episode. Thanks to you he will lose most of it."

"Let's open the bubbly." When he had popped the cork and everyone had a glass he said "Here's to adventure. I really do not know what would have happened if Ellis had not heard about those kippers – and of course if Vaila and Ellis had not become so fond of each other that he returned to Orkney for a holiday. You two, now have a most appropriate reward for your good deeds, if I am not mistaken!"

This time Vaila did not blush. After all why should she mind that they all knew how she felt?

The end.

Postscript.

They stood, as Ellis had suggested, in the middle of the Ring of Brodgar. Vaila still did not understand why he wanted them to be there, but he had told her he hoped it would prove magical. She hoped so too, as she tried to forget he was going home the next day.

He felt the wind around them and thought he could hear its encouraging message, one that would have been repeated down millennia.

Turning to her he kissed her and asked "Will you marry me?" She flung her arms round him "Yes, yes, yes, yes, YES!"

When they eventually got back in the car, they looked at each other grinning. "You were right Ellis, this place is magical." She paused, then "Now I am to be your wife, you have definitely won our bet."

"Oh yes, I had forgotten about that. But you never told me what my prize would be."

"I knew the moment we made the bet but I didn't dare tell you; I thought it might put you off. Anyway you have just claimed your prize - it's me!"

Early in the following spring the small pass door of the prison swung open and a young man stepped out. He had fair hair cut short. His face was pale and his clothes, though not the best quality were neat, and looked as if they had at least been well cared for. He carried a hold all.

He was greeted by his mother. He kissed her and looked at her for several moments with a smile on his face.

"I do not wish to go in there again." He said.

"But you did get time off for good behavior."

"Yes, but let's not talk about that. So how are you?"

"Fine, though I am not used to living here. Still your Father has helped me settle in. He is still cross with you, but he is coming round. What do you want to do now?"

"A good coffee and a really sweet cake. That would be nice. Then you can tell me all that has happened."

When seated in a pleasant coffee shop he said "Well what's the news?"

"I have something which I could show you but I'm not sure if you will want to see it. It is a copy of a recent 'Orcadian' it has pictures of a big wedding." She looked at him with a question on her face.

"Mum, I can guess – its Vaila isn't it? I presume she married Ellis Mackenzie?"

"Yes."

"I am over her now. I hoped he would marry her; they are well matched and now she is married it sort of draws that part of my life to a close too. Let me see it."

When she gave it to him he was surprised to see so much made of the ceremony at St Magnus cathedral, with half page pictures. But then it was the first double wedding, so the paper said, to take place in Orkney. Hal and Inga were married at the same service, and both couples were popular in the islands.

He laughed. "I see Vaila and Ellis are going to Italy on honeymoon. No guesses as to where – he'll want to visit Pompeii. I think she is going to have to get used to trailing round archeological sites!"

He got up from the table with the paper in his hand. He crossed the room, gave it to the staff, telling them to bin it.

Returning to his mother he said "Time to start again. There must be lots of money making possibilities round here and pretty girls just waiting for me too! Let's go home."